I settled down in my sleeping bag, giving myself a few minutes with the battery-powered lamp and Elizabeth Gaskell. I wouldn't keep the light on long, since that might tip someone off that the bus was occupied instead of just parked. The curtains shut out everything but my little domain, where each item had a place and stayed in it.

When I put my book away, I felt a moment's concern that Pigpen might come back after a bottle or two of wine. But the cardboard would keep him from reaching through to the door lock and I had a knife nearby. When I first began living the vagabond life, I was torn between the freedom to go anywhere, escape anything, and the apparent vulnerability of a person with no house around them. As time went on I realized I was much safer in the bus than tied down to an address, where anybody who knows where to look for you can find you.

As it turned out, my concerns about Pigpen Murphy were groundless. Not too long after Elizabeth Gaskell had sent me into my usual deep sleep, he became incapable of putting his hand through any more windows.

At least, not during this lifetime.

NORTHEAST COLORADO BOOKMOBILE SERVICES
325 WEST 7th STREET
WRAY, COLORADO 80758

MURDER IN A NICE NEIGHBORHOOD

Lora Roberts

3NECBS0072501K

FAWCETT GOLD MEDAL • NEW YORK

NORTHEAST COLORADO BOOKMOBILE SERVICES
325 WEST 7th STREET

For Merry, Ruth, Susan, Victoria,
with affectionate gratitude.

Sale of this book without a front cover may be unauthorized. If this book is coverless, it may have been reported to the publisher as "unsold or destroyed" and neither the author nor the publisher may have received payment for it.

A Fawcett Gold Medal Book
Published by Ballantine Books
Copyright © 1994 by Lora Roberts Smith

All rights reserved under International and Pan-American Copyright Conventions. Published in the United States by Ballantine Books, a division of Random House, Inc., New York, and simultaneously in Canada by Random House of Canada Limited, Toronto.

Library of Congress Catalog Card Number: 94-94033

ISBN 0-449-14891-2

Manufactured in the United States of America

First Edition: June 1994

10 9 8 7 6

1

I had the side door open on my '69 VW microbus, enjoying the sun's last gasp for the day. I was reading Elizabeth Gaskell's *Life of Charlotte Brontë* and eating a Bartlett pear. The bus stood on the curbside of a giant Monterey pine that shaded part of San Francisquito Creek, Palo Alto's border. It was one of my favorite spots. Across the creek, the sunset spilled over me through a west-facing gap in the trees. The sunrise would do the same on the opposite, street side of the bus tomorrow.

The pear's fragrance mingled with the resiny aroma of pine and a drift of scent from someone's roses across the street. The evening air was crisp enough to downplay the smell of dog residue that blanketed the creek banks. All the dogs in the neighborhood got their walkies there.

In the quiet, I could hear the twilight songs of the finches, and the wood doves crashing around in the oaks, looking for roosting spots. Elizabeth Gaskell's well-bred Victorian horror at the pathetic details of life among the Brontës was, for some reason, soothing. There was little but core left on the pear when I heard footsteps coming along the pavement.

Being approached when I'm alone always makes me nervous. But I didn't lift my eyes from my book. It was a defense against living out in the middle of things, instead of in a house like the tidy bungalows that line the streets north of downtown Palo Alto. I sometimes felt like a mime, going through invisible doors, establishing invisible boundaries to secure some imagined privacy. Occasionally it worked.

This time it didn't. The man, if he could be dignified by such a classification, came to a stop in front of me. I held the book closer to my face, but he was still there just past the margins. Even though he didn't smell as bad as he usually did, the odor was strong enough to make the smellee want immediate access to a clothespin.

"So, babe. Whatcha doin' tonight?"

I turned a page in my book, still not looking up. The unsavory apparition who addressed me was called Pigpen Murphy on the street—an apt name. Judging from what showed in my peripheral vision, he had recently visited the Goodwill Store. He wore huge, shiny brown wing tips in place of the cracked, broken monstrosities of the past. Nearly submerged in the general effluvia was the faint aroma of mothballs, another indicator that he had not long occupied the loudly checked trousers that ballooned over his new shoes.

The *tout ensemble* was unexpected enough, in conjunction with Pigpen Murphy, that I lifted my eyes briefly from my book—a strategic error.

"You like my new threads?" He struck a preening pose, brushing at the worn vinyl of a brown flight jacket that contrived to look jaunty on his shambling figure. He might have been over six feet tall if he'd stood up straight. But life and drink had bowed him until his head peered out from between his shoulders like a small, inquisitive animal perched on two boulders. Sparse tufts of orangey-red hair circled his scalp and made individual roofs over his eyes.

"Groovy," I assured him, returning my eyes to my book. Experience had taught me that just to reply to one of Pigpen's remarks was tantamount to declaring undying love, in his strange brain. He settled beside me in the doorway of the bus, all two hundred fifty unlovely pounds of him.

"You need to look good when you got a good job," he observed portentously. "I'm goin' somewhere now, Sully. I got money and new clothes. Shit—I might even get me a

2

room at the Carver Arms—for a month. What say, wild mama? Wanna head over to Safeway and pick up a bottle?"

"No," I said, not looking up. It wasn't just his nasty smell that made my insides clench. I don't like men crowding me, threatening me.

He was silent for a minute. I could smell the reek of wine on him and knew he'd already started his evening's potations.

"What is it, I'm not good enough? Nobody's good enough for Miss High and Mighty Sullivan, is that it?" He wasn't yelling, but it wouldn't be long before he was.

"I'm celibate, Mr. Murphy. Everybody knows that."

"Fancy word for queer, ain't it? Me 'n' Alonso been talking about you. Tryin' to figure out what makes a woman act this way." He edged closer, intensifying the olfactory distress. "Me, I said I could warm you up good. You don't look half-bad when I'm drunk, and I'll be drunk pretty soon."

He was drunk already. I closed my book carefully and got to my feet, standing in the doorway of the microbus. I can do that without ducking, since I'm just shy of five-two.

"Enjoy yourself," I said, as pleasantly as I could, controlling the tremor in my voice. "But don't come back here. I'm not interested in what you're offering."

"The hell with that!" Pigpen stood, too, planting both his shiny wing tips on the pavement. As soon as he lifted off from the bus, I slammed the door shut. I hadn't counted on his hand being in the way.

After he removed it, slightly battered, there was no problem. While I locked the door and pulled the curtains shut, Pigpen howled inventive Irish curses. Though I knew he was well anesthetized by alcohol, I slid the window open and offered him the contents of my first-aid kit. It was a mistake. He reached right through the window, and it wasn't first aid he was after. When I bit him, the sour taste of his filthy thumb nearly made me gag. I was careful not to break the skin.

3

I got the window shut while he nursed the bite, but seconds later his fist smashed spitefully through it.

Since the curtains were closed, most of the glass stayed outside. I was a little put out at having to sweep it all up before I left in the morning—broken glass wasn't allowed in my favorite parking spot. But the smashed window was Pigpen's swan song; he stumbled off toward El Camino—heading, most likely, for his hangout by the railroad tracks, to find his buddy Alonso and that bottle from Safeway. His rantings were audible for a while, drifting off down the creek.

I knocked the rest of the window glass onto the street and taped a piece of cardboard from the back of a drawing pad into the frame. The pear core went into a sack for the compost bin. I brushed my teeth in my little sink, squatted over the plastic bucket (covering it tightly when I was done, of course), and pulled out the bed that fills the back of the bus.

It was peaceful again, just the noise of a few late crickets and the distant sound of cars on Middlefield Road. I settled down in my sleeping bag, giving myself a few minutes with the battery-powered lamp and Elizabeth Gaskell. I wouldn't keep the light on long, since that might tip someone off that the bus was occupied instead of just parked. The curtains shut out everything but my little domain, where each item had a place and stayed in it.

When I put my book away, I noticed the duct tape and felt a moment's concern that Pigpen might come back after a bottle or two of wine had drowned the pain from his last visit. But the cardboard would keep him from reaching through to the door lock, and I had a knife nearby. When I first began living the vagabond life, I was torn between the freedom to go anywhere and escape anything, and the apparent vulnerability of a person with no house around them. As time went on I realized I was much safer in the bus than tied down to an address, where anybody who knows where to look for you can find you. Nothing had ever happened to contradict that assumption.

4

As it turned out, my concerns about Pigpen Murphy were groundless. Not too long after Elizabeth Gaskell had sent me into my usual deep sleep, he became incapable of putting his hand through any more windows.

At least, not during this lifetime.

2

IN October, in the Bay Area, nights get cold. The sun was pleasantly warm the next morning, however, heating the bus through the yellow curtains before I crawled out of my sleeping bag.

I used the plastic bucket again. I would empty it at the first construction Porta-potty I drove past on my daily rounds. The houses of Palo Alto are constantly being remodeled, so there's no shortage of Porta-potties. I often took advantage of them, and of the library bathrooms, and of course the shower after I swim.

The bus has many amenities, not the least of which is running water, as long as I keep the water tank beneath the little sink filled. It doesn't matter that it's cold. After washing, I put on three layers of clothes, pushed the curtains back, and sat at the table that folds up in front of the backseat. I ate an orange from a bagful I'd collected out of the dumpster behind Mollie Stone's Market, and a bowl of granola with the last of the quart of milk I'd bought the day before. The sun poured in. It was a lovely morning, clear and promising the warmth of Indian summer.

I had work to do that day at the Senior Center and in the main library, but there was no hurry. The library didn't open until ten o'clock, and I wasn't due at the Senior Center until after two. Actually, one of the best elements of the vagabond life is that there's rarely any hurry. I made a cup of tea, using the fancy immersion heater I'd bought myself last Christmas with the proceeds of a sale to *Young Mother's Story*—"My Husband Wanted Me To Be a Nun"—and let my thoughts drift.

There was a tap on the street-side window next to me. It was Old Mackie, making his daily trip downtown with his shopping cart. The cart was piled with Old Mackie's treasures: warm coats, a spare pair of tennis shoes in a K mart box, neat bags of empty cans and bottles, a bedroll of bedraggled blankets, a foam pillow in a loudly flowered case, and right in front for easy access, a tightly capped jug discreetly hidden in a brown bag.

I slid the window open and handed him an orange. "Morning," I said, making sure he had a firm grip on the orange. Old Mackie got the shakes pretty badly in the mornings. "How are things?"

His head wobbled back and forth, and it was a minute before I realized this was more than the shakes. "Big mess," he said finally. There weren't many teeth left in his mouth, so it was hard to understand him sometimes. "Right underneath."

I frowned, and then remembered the broken glass. "Yeah, there is," I told him. "No real harm done, though."

He gave me a look I couldn't quite interpret. "If you say so," he mumbled and coughed up a huge gob, which he expectorated politely to one side. Spending nights beneath a bush on the creek bank, foam pillow or no, was hard on Old Mackie. On an impulse, I offered him a cup of tea.

He wouldn't take it, which surprised me. Normally he enjoys sitting in the bus with me. He covets the bus. It's no wonder.

"Big mess." He shook his head some more.

I felt a little huffy, like he was casting aspersions on my housekeeping. "The whisk broom will take care of it."

Old Mackie stared at me and started shaking all over. He shook until I began to wonder if I should get him to the hospital, if he was having a stroke. Then noises came from his mouth, and I realized he was laughing.

So hard, in fact, he couldn't speak. He stood there, shaking and pointing one knobby old finger at me, and finally he gave up trying to talk and wheeled his shopping cart away, his shoulders heaving all the way down the block.

I looked around at the inside of the bus, neat as a pin, and felt like saying "Humph!" Instead, I got out the whisk broom and dustpan and opened up the side door.

This morning the air wasn't quite so delightful; there was a waft of sewerish aroma that the pines couldn't overcome. Squatting at the curb, I used the whisk broom to get all the bits of glass into a tidy pile.

The dark stains that congealed in rivers next to the front tire didn't make an impression at first; I wrote them off as old oil leaks. But when I bent farther to get right under the bus, I realized they weren't oil.

Pigpen's face peered out of the jumble of his clothes beneath the bus; it was a wonder his signature smell hadn't alerted me to him. I could see the gleam of his open eyes, and his mouth was twisted as it had been when he'd tried to keep me from closing the bus door. The dark, shiny rivers came from underneath his head. They had coagulated in a parody of motion. The wide eyes, too, were still, filmed over as if smeared with Vaseline. A breeze ruffled the scanty hair above them.

I found myself holding on to one of the bay trees that grew at the edge of the creek, hanging over the twenty-foot bank that forms the sides of the ravine while my stomach tried to come out through my throat. Empty at last, I staggered back to the bus and rinsed my mouth. I took my knapsack from its hiding place and followed old Mackie's route downtown. The closest pay phone was at the 7-Eleven.

I got a cup of tea in the store, even though all the hot liquids at those places taste like coffee. I took my Styrofoam cup out to the pay phone and called the police. The woman at the other end wanted me to stay on the line until the of-

7

ficers came. I gave her the location of my bus once more and hung up.

There was a rest room in the Laundromat next to the 7-Eleven, and I needed it. Carrying the still-hot cup of tea, I walked back to the creek. The uniforms got there before me.

3

"YOU the one that called us?" The cop who approached me was a woman. I took that as a good omen.

"Yes." I gulped what was left of the tea; most of it had sloshed out as I lurched down the sidewalk. "That's my bus."

I stared at it longingly. There were cops all over it—inside, beneath where the remains of Pigpen Murphy languished, all around the outside. I wished I'd gotten a chance to empty the plastic bucket. That's how confused I was—catastrophe surrounded me, and I was worried that I'd look like a bad housekeeper.

The cop stared at me curiously, and I realized I had to pull myself together. People of the vagabond persuasion are at grave risk in any dealings with the police. I, especially, could end up in big trouble.

"You live in the vehicle? Alone?" She was writing things down. I had a hysterical impulse for my own notebook. I would write down what she said; she would write down what I said. A dreadful symmetry would ensue.

"I travel," I corrected her. "Yes, alone."

"Did you know the deceased?"

Some of the superfluity of cops were stringing cords

around the bus and over the curb to the creek bank. From where I stood I could see under the bus. Pigpen's immense shoes pointed skyward as if he were waiting his cue to roll out and join some macabre circus.

"I didn't know him," I said finally. "He came around. His last name was Murphy."

"First name?"

"Beats me." The sun was getting warmer. I took off the top layer—a red-and-white-striped poncho with a hood. "He was called Pigpen Murphy."

She wrote it down solemnly. I guessed she hadn't been within smelling distance of the corpse.

"Can you tell me what happened?"

One of the men cops materialized next to me. Both he and the woman watched me with remote sympathy. I didn't feel at my intellectual best, but I tried to tell the story coherently anyway.

"Last night," I said, "he came around. He'd done it before. He was not the kind of person to take a hint. I finally got it across that I wanted him to leave, and he left."

The cops exchanged glances. "How did you get it across?" The man spoke for the first time. His nameplate said "Rucker." The woman's said "Horton." I spent a few seconds memorizing those names while I got my thoughts in order.

"I shut the door of the bus." Reluctantly, because I knew they would find the evidence when they pored over his body, I added, "His hand was in the way at the time."

"You shut the door on his hand." Horton might have smiled, if she hadn't been in uniform. "And you said he went away."

"First he slammed his fist through my window," I said, scrupulously sticking to facts. "I had to bite him on the thumb, too. Then he left, going toward El Camino. I taped up the window, locked my doors, and went to sleep. I sleep very soundly."

Now they were both writing in their little notebooks.

Horton used a ballpoint. Rucker used a mechanical pencil. My fingers itched to hold the razor-point felt tip I prefer.

"Did you hear anything in the night?" Rucker was really not bad-looking for a cop. He was young—mid-twenties, at a guess. Still downy in my opinion. It's not that I think thirty-four is old, but the past few years have contained a lot of hard mileage, for me and my VW. Rucker looked as if the river of life had yet to sweep him under. He was tall, broad-shouldered, surfer-boy blond.

I nearly laughed at his question. "Not anymore," I said. "If I woke up every time a car went by or the train whistles blew, I'd never get any sleep. I don't wake up unless someone touches the bus."

"And did anyone?" Horton held her pen poised.

"Not last night." I looked again at the huddled shape beneath the bus. "Listen—what did he die of?"

They exchanged glances. "We don't know as yet," Horton said smoothly. "We're waiting for the detectives to get here. Please tell me how you found the body."

I made as short a story as I could of it, leaving out Old Mackie. There was no reason to set a pack of policemen breathing down his venerable neck. I could still see my whisk broom and dustpan lying on the ground beside the bus's open door. As further corroboration, and out of devilment, I mentioned the episode of emptying my guts into the creek. One unlucky uniform had to climb down through the poison oak and scrape up whatever he could find of my effluvia.

That was the high point of my morning. They wouldn't let me have the bus back. I found a tree a little ways down the block and leaned against it. At last the detectives came.

All of them seethed around like ants trying to drag home a cookie. It might have been entertaining if it hadn't been my bus they were taking apart, and potentially my ass at stake. I spent a few minutes longing like crazy to rewind all this madness and start my life again just before Pigpen had come along the previous evening. If I'd known, I would have driven off five minutes before he'd shown up, and parked in one of the other spots I'd cultivated around Palo Alto.

At last one of the non-uniforms came over to the tree I had staked out and squatted down for a talk. He'd glanced over Horton's notes. I'd watched him through the back window of the bus, rummaging in my file box. That had bothered me—a lot. Private papers are not meant to be read by any bozo who comes along.

"I've been through your statement, Ms. Sullivan." He shuffled some papers he held in his hands.

"That's not all you've been through."

"I beg your pardon?"

"You should." I unclenched my hands and folded them in my lap. "You didn't even bother to show me a search warrant before you turned my bus inside out."

He had the grace to redden a little. He didn't look like a cop at all—maybe half a foot taller than I am, with a stocky build and a lot of curly, uncombed hair in a nondescript shade between brown and gray. The fact that he wore granny glasses was disarming, somehow. But still, he'd snooped in my files.

"In cases of violent death, we tend to examine everything with a fine-tooth comb. You're a suspect, Ms. Sullivan. Maybe you haven't understood that."

Anger and fear have an unfortunate effect on me. I turn into a raving smartass. It took a minute before I could be sure I had my mouth under control. Deep breathing helps.

"May I see your identification?" He scowled, but he handed it to me. I took my time with it, breathing deeply and exerting control over my emotions. His name was Paul Drake, which would have been funny under other circumstances. I browsed through the rest of the leather folder that held his ID, despite his smothered protest. There was a credit card slip from a gas station, a phone message that said "Call S. 555-5578," and a small, blurry photograph that showed several indeterminate people sitting along a restaurant bench, their arms around each other.

I handed the leather folder back and he shoved it into his

hip pocket. He wore jeans, red high-tops, and a tweed sport coat that had seen better days. Really, he wasn't much better dressed than one of the nattier street people. I didn't know why he was staring at me. I am fond of vegetables and had used fabric paint to duplicate some of my favorites on the gray sweatshirt that had cost $1.84 at Goodwill.

"Your identification, Ms. Sullivan." He held out his hand, and I cannily gave him my naked driver's license, with no supporting documentation. He took it over to the closest cruiser and reached in to use the radio. Waiting for the inevitable, I got to my feet.

"You have a couple of citations for vagrancy on your record, Ms. Sullivan," Drake said when he came back. "Have to ask you to wait in the car for me, please."

They took my keys, and I perched on the backseat of the cruiser, maintaining as much dignity as was possible in the circumstances. People were gathered on the sidewalks, coming out of their nice little bungalows and restored Victorians. They stared at me and at the police, who were finally scraping Pigpen out from under my bus. I thought about how long it would be before I could park overnight in that neighborhood again. It helped to divert me from the real fear that occupied my mind—how long it would be before I would even see my bus. Vagabonds are notoriously easy marks to fasten on when questions of guilt and retribution come around.

Drake hovered over the uniforms, who were having some difficulty getting Pigpen's remains out from under the bus. In my increasingly light-headed state, the whole operation began to resemble commedia dell'arte. When at last they got Pigpen onto a stretcher, and those shoes disappeared into the ambulance, I nearly burst into applause.

The impulse to levity dried up when Drake came back with one of the uniforms, and they climbed into the cruiser. "We'll talk at the office," Drake said, barely glancing at me.

"What about my bus?" Among the crowd at the curb, I

noticed Old Mackie, muttering and shaking and eyeing the bus with his usual yearning.

"It's the least of your worries right now, ma'am." Drake faced front again and we made a wide U-turn, heading toward downtown. By craning my neck I could see my bus, still surrounded by a swarm of uniforms, like bees around the hiving queen.

4

I cooled my heels for a good couple of hours in a small room with no windows and no doors. It was unpleasantly reminiscent of a cell, which made me a claustrophobic wreck. They'd printed me, which added to my nervousness. Besides, my bladder was responding to all this negative stimulus by letting me know that I needed the bathroom again. After losing my breakfast all over the creek bank, I felt weak, although not in the least hungry. Waves of panic alternated with the memory of Pigpen's glazed eyes. I wondered about the third degree that undoubtedly awaited me. Why was it taking so long? What were they up to, those minions of the law?

There was a time in the distant past when I truly believed that policemen were my friends. That was before various events showed me differently. I now knew that policemen weren't anyone's friends, although some of them could be rented as friends if you had money or influence, or both. In Palo Alto, I'd always gotten pretty fair treatment from the cops, partly due to my mobility. I was careful never to park too long in one place, to keep a low profile, to retreat to the campgrounds at Butano or Portola State

Park at the first sign of interest. I had learned a lot after being stopped for vagrancy a couple of times in Southern California, when I was just starting out on the vagabond life. I had thought it was all under control. And there were so many more available targets among the street people that I'd managed to avoid attention.

Not anymore, obviously. Even if I could miraculously elude any trouble brought on by this unsavory event, I would be branded, easily visible. And I'd grown to like Palo Alto. I'd gone so far as to put down roots in the three years I'd been living on its streets. Always a mistake for a vagabond.

It must have been after ten o'clock before I was ushered into the inner sanctum. Drake's office was of the cubbyhole persuasion. When we were both squeezed in there wasn't much room left over. He plopped a cup of coffee down in front of me and took a sip of his own.

"It isn't poisoned," he said finally. I hadn't touched my cup.

"I don't drink coffee." I was examining the walls of his office, looking for clues about how to deal with him, with all the ranks of officialdom. It was pretty obvious that if the police felt like it, they could just write scapegoat all over me and call it quits.

Drake sighed heavily and left the room. He came back after a minute with another Styrofoam cup. The smell of Red Zinger filled the room. I really don't like it either, but at least it wasn't coffee, and the warm cup was comforting.

"According to your story," Drake said, taking another belt of coffee, "you had a disagreement with this Murphy last night and he went away, relatively unharmed. Sometime during the night his dead body turned up under the car you were sleeping in." He looked up from the papers he'd been reading. "That's enough to get you in trouble right there. No camping allowed on the streets of Palo Alto."

"I wasn't camping." The defense came automatically. I pretended to sip some of the Red Zinger. "I meant to go up to Portola State Park, but I was overcome by sleepiness and just pulled over."

"Sure, sure." Drake wasn't buying it, obviously.

"I should have taken my chances with that winding road," I added, putting a little more straw into my bricks.

Drake leaned back in his chair. "These other vagrancy infractions," he said softly. "Do you have a permanent address?"

"I have a post office box," I said after a minute. "I have a bank account. If I were living on a boat no one would give me any trouble. What's the law against living in a bus?"

"No law." He looked uncomfortable.

"Just isn't allowed in nice Palo Alto, huh? I'll have to get a slot in the trailer park. Except—there aren't any trailer parks here, are there? They'd be too tacky for these parts."

He shot me a look, and I shut up. Something in me wanted to antagonize him—the stupid part of me, I guess.

"There are, actually." He crushed his cup and threw it away. "Trailer parks. I live in one of them."

This was interesting information. I tried to fit it into my preconceptions about him, and couldn't. "There's always Redwood City," I muttered. The Styrofoam cup cracked in my hand, and a little Red Zinger dripped onto my sweatshirt. "This cup is politically incorrect, you know."

He took a deep breath. "We know, Ms. Sullivan. But it would be even worse for the environment to throw them out without using them first."

I set the cup back on his desk, leak and all. "Well, it's been nice chatting with you. Are you finished asking questions?"

"You're not going anywhere."

"You charging me?"

For a minute he just glared. "Ms. Sullivan—" He ran his hands through his hair, giving himself an even wilder aspect. "You don't seem like the kind of woman who usually hangs out with the street people. What's the story?"

"There's no story." For lack of anything better to do with

my hands, I picked up the cup of Red Zinger again. "I don't hang out with anyone. Not them, not you."

"You knew who this Murphy was," he said, scanning the report again. "You obviously buy into that life-style."

"What life-style are we discussing?"

"You have no fixed address," he pointed out, pawing through the papers that strewed his desk as if the Dead Sea Scrolls were hidden there somewhere. "The street people know you as someone who keeps to herself, who carries it to an extreme, even for them. You—"

"Wait a minute." It was getting warm in the room. I peeled off the gray sweatshirt with the vegetables and was down to my final layer, a pink-flowered long underwear top originally owned by a woman of immense proportions, judging from the slack that existed between my hands and the ends of the sleeves. I rolled them up four times before they cleared my wrists. "You've been asking after me on the street?"

"Field work," he said mildly. His glasses flashed when he glanced at my chest. I could have kept my sweatshirt on, but I didn't see any reason why I should roast to preserve Detective Drake from the necessity of admiring my figure. I don't choose my fashions to enhance the body—in fact, the reverse.

"So what did you find out?" There was another reason why I'd have to move on. When this was over with, even if I were cleared of complicity in Pigpen's death, there would still be people with long memories for trouble who'd be wary of me. The underground community is very tight. For those living on the fringes of society, they have a touching faith in the law. If the law fingered me as a killer, if my innocence were never proved, I would be doubly outcast.

"Not much," he said, giving me a look. "Rucker asked around—he knows a few of them. You're considered friendly, but not matey. You have some nice things for someone in your economic stratum, it's been noticed."

I hoped that the police were guarding my van.

"Well," I said as nonchalantly as I could, "there you have it. My life in a nutshell. Any more questions?"

"Where did the nice things come from?" Drake watched me, his face impassive, his glasses catching the light.

"I earned them." The Red Zinger was cooler now, and actually more palatable. "I work, Detective Drake. This is America, after all."

"What do you work at?" The skin around his mouth tightened.

"I'm a writer." The word made me glance around absent-mindedly for my notebook, which I had slipped into the big carryall. At least the police hadn't got their mitts on it. "As you may know, writers make on the average less than seven thousand dollars a year. Hence, the van. I earn enough to be comfortable in it. I couldn't begin to afford to live anywhere else unless I hang out under the El Camino underpass with the rest of the bums."

"What do you write?" He didn't back off, which was the result I had hoped for with the disclosure of my meager income. Though I prefer not to mention such vulgar topics, there's no denying that most people will avoid someone whose income is too low even to register on the tax tables.

"I am a literary craftsman." His expression didn't change. "I carry on the tradition of the scribe. I write anything, anywhere, for anyone."

"Like who?"

"*Grit. True Confessions. Sewanee Review. Police Story. Family Circle.* The *Mercury News.* The *LA Times. Organic Gardener. Bon Appetit.*"

He wrote them all down, wrinkling his forehead over a couple of them.

"If you're published, how come you don't make more?"

I said patiently, "There aren't many magazines that pay a living wage, and I haven't yet managed to crack them. Just because I write a great article doesn't mean anyone is obliged to buy it, although I am doing better each year. To rent an apartment around here you need first and last month's rent and a hefty deposit. I couldn't find a room in someone else's house for what I earn." I sat up a little straighter. "And if I could, I wouldn't. My life suits me fine, Detective Drake. I have everything I need, and enough leisure—"

The office door opened. "Paolo. Sorry to be late."

Drake waved permission to enter. "Hey, don't worry about it, Bruno. This is Ms. Sullivan. About the Murphy killing."

The other man perched on one edge of Drake's desk, examining me with real sympathy in his tender brown eyes. "Bruno Morales," he said, extending a hand. I shook it before I realized I was going to. "How are you feeling, Ms. Sullivan? That was not a nice thing for you to find."

I felt warmed through by this simple little speech. "I got sick all over the creek bank," I confided artlessly. And then thought, Was that me?

"So I heard." He turned his gaze on Drake, who seemed to squirm a little. "You're not giving Ms. Sullivan a hard time, are you, Paolo?"

"Of course not." Drake was defensive. "She hasn't given a very coherent account of herself, though."

"How can you say that?" Morales waved some papers he held in his hand. "All witnesses should be so succinct." He turned to me, smiling again. "Admirable, Ms. Sullivan."

"Thank you." I had the wild thought that Morales had brought a kind of tea-party atmosphere with him. Any minute now he was going to offer a plate of little sandwiches and ask me how my family was.

"Is there someone you would like to call?" His nice face was worried. "The clerk says you haven't even called a lawyer yet."

"Do I need one?" I knew a lawyer to call. But like most of the world, he was hung up on payment. And I didn't care for the kind of payment he had suggested in the past.

Morales considered it. "No, not exactly," he said at last. "We don't really have grounds enough to charge anyone yet." He bent his limpid gaze on me. "You wouldn't hap-

18

pen to know where Mr. Murphy spent most of his time, would you?"

I stared back gravely into those warm brown eyes. "I never visited his pied-à-terre, if that's what you mean."

His face relaxed a bit. Of course they knew where Murphy hung out. They'd been talking to all the street people. Those folks wouldn't tell more than they could get away with, but Murphy was probably no more popular with them than I was.

Drake leaned back in his chair, not quite smiling. I glanced from Morales to him. "Is this your usual method?" They both stared at me blankly. "Good cop, bad cop? He"— I pointed to Drake—"scares the suspect, and you come along and apply balm."

Neither of them bothered to reply. They chased me around the same old territory for a little while longer, and then a distraction came up. The surfer boy that I'd seen earlier came in.

"Rucker." Paul Drake stood up to greet him, taking the inevitable sheaf of papers from him. "What's new?"

Rucker looked at me, hesitant, and Drake gestured him into speech.

"Talked to an old guy they call Mackie. He said he walked past Ms. Sullivan's vehicle early this morning." Rucker glanced at me, both apologetic and accusing. "Says he spoke with Ms. Sullivan here and tried to tell her there was a body under her bus, but she didn't seem to catch on. She was eating breakfast, he said."

All the masculine eyes in the room were fixed on me. "So that's what he meant," I said. "I thought he was just talking about the broken glass."

"This man could be a witness in your favor, Ms. Sullivan. Why didn't you tell us about your encounter with him?" Morales shook his head sorrowfully over my lapse.

"Old Mackie is not exactly the most reliable character witness," I pointed out. "And I didn't think you should be pestering him. He's old and—and not well."

"Drunk as a loon, he was," Rucker said bluntly. With

him in the doorway, the little office was crowded and hot. I didn't mind the lack of space—I'm used to that. But the heat made me wish I'd put on something short-sleeved that morning under the long underwear top. I don't mind cold too much, but heat bothers me.

"We expect a full account from you of every little thing that happened to you from your meeting with Murphy last night on," Drake said softly, his eyes hard behind his wire-rims. "Anything else you've neglected to tell us?"

I thought for a minute. "I had an orange for breakfast," I said innocently. "But then, you probably know that already."

Morales's mouth twitched, but Drake wouldn't loosen up. "I mean it, Ms. Sullivan," he snarled. "If you're not the guilty party in this whole setup, does it occur to you that someone planted a dead body right where it would do you the most harm?"

There it was in the open, a thought I'd been suppressing rather successfully. "Actually," I said, "it has. And if you want to know who would do that to a sweet young thing like me, the answer is—I don't know."

I couldn't keep the tremble out of my voice, and it seemed to occur to Drake for the first time that he'd been hot-boxing me for a quite a while.

"Let's take a break," he said gruffly. "The ladies' room is that way—the women's room, or whatever," he added to my raised eyebrows. "Right next to the canteen. We'll meet you there in a few minutes."

He didn't have to add that he didn't want me to run away. In any case, I had nowhere to go, and no way to get there.

It was blissful to be alone for a while. I attended to my bodily functions, which were by now quite insistent. The clerk had given me back my big bag, after searching it and removing my Swiss army knife. But I had toothpaste and a hairbrush, and my sandalwood soap in a plastic bag. I washed my hands and brushed my hair, put the vegetable sweatshirt back on, and eased the door open. I was at the end of the hall, and there was an exit right across from me. I looked at it for a minute, wondering if the alarm really would sound. Finally I went on into the canteen.

5

THE canteen was full of plastic chairs and Formica-topped tables. Uniformed cops clustered around one table. A man and woman sat across from each other at another, holding hands as if there was nothing else on earth to hold onto. Most of the tables were empty.

There was a machine that gave various forms of hot drinks. I dialed up a cup of hot chocolate, dumped some of the powdered creamer into it, and took it over to the table in the corner where Drake and Morales sat, watching me.

"So," I said with breezy cheerfulness—or tried to—"isn't it about time for me to be heading out? Hate to keep you longer."

They were still watching me, Morales looking sober, Drake with the fluorescent light making blanks of his wire-rims. "Sit down," he said softly. "Please."

I sat. Drake leaned forward, and I could see his eyes. They were gray—the pale, cold gray of frozen sidewalks. I had a sick feeling, as if they had at last discovered me to be a fraud, as if they were getting my cell ready for me.

"We've just gotten a report," he said, "from a man who admitted to drinking with Murphy from eight-thirty last night until after ten." He paused, thinking this should mean something to me, I guess. I sat there, not having been commanded to do anything else, letting the coldness spread inside me.

"According to him," Drake went on after a moment, "Murphy had a lot of money on him, in spite of already being drunk. They bought a bottle and drank that, with Murphy bellowing about women and what bitches they were. Then he pulled out another wad of money and said, 'There's more where this came from. I'm asking for a raise, and I'll get it, with what I know!' They bought another bottle, and Murphy drank half of it before he staggered off. The other guy asked where he was going, and he said he was going to the bank."

There was a small silence. I mustered my voice, hoping it would come out normally. "I can see that you believe I am the bank." The words didn't quaver, and I took a breath to go on. "But since there is no currency in which I would have had commerce with Pigpen Murphy, you'll have to look farther afield."

I should have kept my mouth shut. Drake lifted an eyebrow.

"You're an educated woman, Ms. Sullivan. Where did you go to school?"

I had a moment of intense relief, so strong it was almost like a drug. So they hadn't done a complete background check on me—yet, anyway.

"I'm self-taught," I said, striving for a relaxed, unworried tone.

Bruno Morales was still concerned by my speaking ill of the dead.

"Why did you hate Mr. Murphy so much? When you make such a point of your feelings—"

"Hate?" I looked at him, astonished. "I didn't hate him. I just despised him." I looked at them both, wretched judgmental males that they were. "Actually," I went on recklessly, "I despise most men, as a general rule."

They stared at me for a minute, then glanced at each other. "I see," said Drake, finally. His voice was carefully noncommittal.

"I'm not gay, either." I stirred my cocoa and tried not to feel defensive. "I just don't get involved."

They were silent for a moment. "So you didn't get involved with Mr. Murphy?" Bruno Morales had a puzzled crease between his eyebrows.

"Give me credit for a little good taste," I muttered. "No, I had no relationship whatsoever with Murphy, aside from being badgered by him whenever he saw me." I glanced at Drake, unable to read his expression. "Lots of men are like that. They see any solitary woman as available. I wasn't." I thought that over. "I'm not."

"So if a man was insistent enough, bothered you enough, you just might pick up the nearest heavy object and dot him one, is that it?" Drake made the suggestion in a smooth voice, ignoring Morales's distressed cluck.

It took an effort, but I kept my expression blank. "I have never hit anyone over the head," I said shortly. It was the truth, as far as it went.

"Ms. Sullivan." Morales shook his head, concerned. "You have no alibi. You were in the area where the crime was committed—"

"How do you know that?" I remembered his earlier comment. "What if he was killed elsewhere and dumped under my bus?" It was more than surreal to be sitting with policemen, having cocoa that tasted like coffee and discussing the violent death of someone I knew, if only slightly. Time seemed to stretch out, the way it does during intense experiences.

"He was alive when he was shoved beneath your vehicle," Drake said. He leaned back in his chair, as if he were enjoying himself. "Otherwise he wouldn't have bled so much."

"I see." What I saw was the steel jaws of the justice system closing around me. They could make a case against me—they were making it. There was little I could do to stop them. "And you think a woman my size could hit a big guy like Murphy over the head—"

"A woman more likely than a man, if he was conscious," Drake said thoughtfully. "He wouldn't be suspicious of a woman."

"And then drag him over to my bus—for some odd reason—and put him underneath it—"

"She has a point there, Paolo." Morales smiled at me. "If he was killed somewhere along the creek, it would be far easier to tumble him into it, where it might look accidental."

"A strong woman, even if she was short, could drag him that distance," Drake argued. He was enjoying himself—there was something expansive about the way he sipped his coffee. "We know Murphy was setting out to visit someone, and Ms. Sullivan was doubtless the person on his mind."

"So complimentary of you to think so," I murmured, trying to control my panicky breathing. That sense of impending claustrophobia I'd felt in the holding room came back to stifle me. "If your informant is correct, Murphy mentioned the bank. Perhaps he was simply going to use his autoteller card."

Drake stared at me for a minute, and burst into laughter. "We better check up on that, Bruno." He got to his feet, leaving his half-full cup of coffee on the table. "Back to work, eh?" He turned away from the table, and then swung around again. "Oh, here you are, Ms. Sullivan." He tossed my keys onto the table. "You can pick up your other stuff at the front desk. Don't leave town, now. It would look very bad."

The release from tension was almost painful. I stared after Drake, resentful and elated at the same time.

Morales patted my arm. "It's just his way, Ms. Sullivan. But he's right—you must cooperate with us now or you risk being detained. Where will you be staying?"

This was a pitfall I hadn't seen. Morales noticed my hesitation. "You must give the clerk an address, you see," he told me gently. "Perhaps it would be better if you found a hotel room for a while. The Carver Arms—"

I shuddered.

"It's cheap," he insisted. "And we will investigate as quickly as possible."

"I'll find someplace. Can I let you know later?"

He shook his head. "The clerk can make a reservation for you," he said. So much for Mr. Nice Guy. "We will be in touch." He hesitated, and added, "If it would be better, I can have you taken into custody. I think you would prefer the Carver Arms."

"I think you're right." I offered him my hand. "Thanks for your help, Detective Morales."

"Be careful." He shook my hand gently and guided me down the hall toward the front desk. "We don't want anything bad to happen to you, Ms. Sullivan.

It was a nice thought, but it didn't exactly reassure me.

6

THE bus was parked in the underground lot beneath City Hall. Inside it was a stilled maelstrom, where the contents of my life had been whirled through the bureaucracy and, I hoped, come out the other side. I sat in the driver's seat for several minutes, not moving, not really breathing, before I could put the key in the ignition. Carefully, as if guiding an invalid, I drove up the ramp and onto Bryant Street. By the time I got to Channing I was shaking so hard I had to pull over.

For vagabonds, mobility becomes essential. Nothing is as fear-inducing as being deprived of the means of getting away, getting out of town. There was no knowing how close I had come to losing this, to being penned like livestock awaiting its fate. The relief was a euphoria close to panic, especially when I considered that, though I had wheels, I was no longer free. My pen was larger than a cell, but I was tethered within it, my fate still uncertain.

At last I got a grip on myself. Hunger made me light-headed. It was past breakfast, too early for lunch. I gobbled some peanut butter crackers and headed for the library, stopping along the way at a deserted construction site on Cowper to empty the plastic bucket in one of a bevy of Porta-potties. I wondered if the police had seized their opportunity to get a specimen, but that didn't matter, except for the affront to my civil liberties. I was clean, even if the bus, after its intensive search, was not. For the time being, I left the mess alone. I wanted the quiet calm of the library reading room. And murder or no murder, I had a living to make.

Once at my table, with the volumes I needed, I couldn't concentrate. I kept seeing Pigpen Murphy's face, distorted with pain after I shut the door on his hand. If I'd known he was going to die, I might have been kinder.

But I doubt it.

At last I pulled my thoughts back to the research I was doing. I had gotten a go-ahead from *Smithsonian* on a query that dealt with the rowdy little town of Mayfield, which had been gradually overcome and engulfed by Leland Stanford's statelier creation, Palo Alto. As late as yesterday, completing that article and seeing it in print had been my all-encompassing goal. *Smithsonian* paid splendidly, especially compared with *True Story* or *Grit*. It was a credit to be proud of. And once admitted to their coterie of freelancers, a writer had a good chance of selling them another article. I had several ideas composting in the back of my mind.

But I couldn't harness my concentration away from fruitless speculation on this encroaching blot of murder. It didn't help that my current research was a necessary but rather boring perusal of contemporary documents. Bound volumes of the *Mayfield Enterprise* were stacked on the table. I meant to trace the feisty little town's early defiance of Stanford's edicts, and its later capitulation, through the hints and signs that appeared as early as 1897. I worked away doggedly for an hour before realizing that I didn't remember anything I'd read. Finally I returned the volumes to the reference desk.

I drove up Hopkins and made a U-turn, parking beside the Magic Forest, a nice grove of redwoods donated to the city by some arboreal-minded rich person. It took half an hour to tidy the bus. My resentment against the police grew. Why should they have the power to paw through my underwear? Sniggering at my ragged bras was not likely to get them further toward identifying Pigpen Murphy's killer.

After everything was in order I collected the stuff I would need and walked through the Magic Forest to the swimming pool. The lunchtime lap swimmers were leaving, so the lanes were uncrowded. I changed in the women's dressing room, nodding to the regulars with whom I had a passing acquaintance, and went out to submerge my irritation and angst in a good twenty laps.

Afterward I took a shower, not minding that the water came out in a skin-pummeling blast that had the other women wincing and dancing away. I washed my hair and dressed in clean clothes. I swim nearly every day, no matter what the weather. It costs over thirty dollars a month for the tickets, but the shower makes it well worthwhile. And it's nice to be in company with others of my sex. The other women don't even give my faded, second-hand swimsuits a glance.

Feeling more relaxed, I walked out the gate and headed back around the pool toward my van. There was a police car parked behind it.

The cop didn't get out when he spotted me. I slung my bag and rolled-up bundle of wet things into the bus, instead of spreading them on the roof like I usually did for a quick drying session. Nobody hindered me when I got into the driver's seat. When I pulled out, the cop car pulled out. It followed me all the way downtown.

I felt sick again, and underneath that, enraged. Was this my future—constantly being followed by agents of the law?

Boundaries and restrictions chafe us all, but especially those to whom freedom is as necessary as clean water. It galled me to think that I was expected to hunker down in the stale-urine-scented ambience of the Carver Arms and wait for the police to consent to inform me of what they were doing.

The parking lot behind the Senior Center was full, but I managed to get a space on the street. The police car cruised slowly past. I saw the cop inside talking on his radio. I spread my wet things out as well as I could in the sun that came through the bus windows, opening one for ventilation. If anyone started poking around, I could see them from the conference room where my workshop was held.

I was so busy craning around looking for more police persecution that I bumped right into Delores Mitchell as she came out of the Senior Center.

Delores was perfectly dressed, as usual, in her demure little bank-vice-president's suit, with her demure little pumps on. It is a sign of pettiness, I suppose, to find a woman irritating merely because she is younger than you, has an important job, and still finds time to volunteer as a teacher at the Senior Center. She ran a class on financial planning and tax tips that was much more popular than my class. Delores herself was popular; I heard on every side how nice she was, how considerate. Maybe that's what I couldn't forgive.

She gave me her usual sweet, conscientious smile. "Hi, Liz. The ladies were beginning to think you weren't coming. Car trouble?"

"No." Delores drove a BMW, naturally. It was parked right out front, taking up two spaces—her idea of protection for its gleaming red paint. "But isn't that a dent on the passenger door of your car? Shame to see it there—and what's that smudge?"

"On *my* car?" Delores dashed across the sidewalk and I went on into the building, a little guilt mixed with my internal amusement.

I conducted a writing workshop at the Senior Center

twice a week. There are many more qualified than I to undertake this, I hasten to point out, and many of them had. One by one, they'd given it up. The last person to run it, Bridget Montrose, had consented to fill in temporarily, and after she could no longer hack it, had suggested me, and also suggested, bless her, that a small stipend accompany my efforts. This had proved satisfactory to all parties. I enjoyed a steady income, even if it did no more than keep me in postage. And humility is not a bad quality in a writer's workshop leader. I knew markets, for those who wrote for publication, and I enjoyed the stories of those who wrote for themselves. In the past year, we'd all benefited.

The ladies were gathered around the long table in a room off the lobby of the Senior Center, which used to be the police station. I gave some thought to that while I settled myself at the head of the table with the notebook that I keep for the class.

"Are we all here?" I glanced around the table, where six women were seated, instead of the seven I'd expected. They were the most faithful attendees in the history of the world. Only illness or a trip kept them away from the workshop. "Where's Eunice?"

"Didn't you know?" Carlotta Houseman leaned forward from her seat at my right. "Eunice died last Friday, Liz. I thought they'd have told you."

Maybe they had. I hadn't checked my post office box that morning, having other things on my mind. Or maybe they'd just given up. People don't send things in the mail in this telephone age, even if you don't have a phone. They just stop trying to contact you. It has its advantages.

"I'm sorry to hear that." Eunice Giacommetti had been confined to a wheelchair for the past couple of months, but she'd still enjoyed the workshop, and was as careful a listener as you'd want to have, even if she hadn't managed to write much. "Was it another stroke?"

"Her heart, I think," Helen Petrie said vaguely. "After that last stroke, the doctor told her it was just a matter of time."

"It is for all of us," snorted Janet Aronson. She was a big, rawboned woman with iron-gray curls that snapped around her head, and the kind of pale blue eyes that could see through bullshit at forty paces.

"I couldn't get hold of you for the memorial service yesterday, Liz," Vivien Greely said gently. She was looking frail too. Her gnarled fingers gripped the handle of her footed cane. She lived alone, in a rather run-down little bungalow on a huge lot north of University. The cottage in back, even more run-down, was rented to a succession of Stanford students, who gave Vivien a hand when things got beyond her, as they frequently did. One of the students had once scraped together enough cast-off computer equipment to get Vivien started, since keyboarding was easier on her hands than writing with a pen. From there, she'd never looked back.

"Poor Eunice was alone in the house. She should never have stayed there after the stroke. I warned her." Carlotta sounded the tiniest bit complacent. She lived next door to Vivien; Eunice lived around the corner from them. They had all been neighbors for thirty years or more.

"That's the way to go," Janet trumpeted, glaring back at Carlotta. "No one to fuss over you, no one to haul you off to the life-support system. Just one clear call—"

"If we're going to quote Tennyson—" Helen Petrie began.

"We're not." I looked around the table. Freda Vaughn's faded brown eyes had filled with easy tears; she was dabbling at them with an embroidered hanky. Emily Pierce was scribbling in a card, which she signed with a flourish and passed to Vivien.

"Sympathy card. I thought we could all sign it," she announced. "Poor Eunice. A blessed release, I suppose."

"That's right." Carlotta made a little tent with her fingers and looked soulful. "Poor Eunice is beyond suffering now." She shook her head sadly. "She should have sold out when she had the opportunity. They might have been able to save her if she'd had assisted living."

"You're selling, Carlotta?" Emily looked interested. She lived in a different neighborhood, closer to the Lucie Stern Community Center. "What kind of offers did you get, if you don't mind my asking?"

"It is rather confidential at this point." Carlotta preened a little. "But it's a substantial sum. I could move just about anywhere—even the Forum, if I wanted. There's still a chance it will go through." She looked meaningfully at Vivien. "I always say, don't wait until it's too late."

Vivien was unruffled. "I don't want to leave my home, Carlotta. And neither did Eunice." She turned to me. "Are there any exciting manuscripts today, Liz?"

We got down to our reading, but I thought about Eunice while I should have been listening to Carlotta's account of her first encounter with childbirth, some fifty-odd years ago. Eunice had mostly written about her life, too—not with the belligerent vigor Janet used, or the self-satisfaction Carlotta employed, but with modesty and insight. We would miss her contributions to the workshop.

I could see the street from my seat at the table. Delores Mitchell was out there still, anxiously polishing her BMW's door, squinting at the minuscule dent I'd called to her attention. I felt those guilty stirrings again, but when she pulled out a little hand-held vacuum cleaner and began to clean the seats, it evaporated. Neatness is fine, but that was compulsion. Listening to Carlotta, I watched the soles of Delores's nice pumps, which stuck out the passenger door as she worked. I fantasized someone coming along, absently trying to slam the door shut—but that conjured up images of Pigpen, his hand caught in the door, his face contorted. . . .

I took a few deep breaths before I could bring my attention back to Carlotta, hoping her triumphant account of agony endured would distract me from even more unpalatable thoughts.

31

7 _____

THE workshop ended at four P.M., and I bid the ladies farewell, lingering to take on a commission from Vivien. Since she no longer drove, I had gotten in the habit of doing her marketing every week.

"I can manage until day after tomorrow," she said, moving toward the conference room door with her slow, cane-assisted steps. "Is that okay with you?"

"Sure," I said, hoping I wouldn't be arrested by then. "I'll stop by with your stuff around nine-thirty or so on Thursday."

"And you'll stay for tea," she insisted. I held the front door of the Senior Center for her.

"I'd be delighted." We moved into the lobby, as I matched my steps to hers.

"Mrs. Greely!"

Vivien stopped and smiled at the tall man who'd hailed her.

"Why, Mr. Ramsey." She blinked a little flirtatiously. The man smiled at her with the great warmth that some people learn in their professions—lawyers and politicians, for instance. "How nice to see you again."

"My pleasure," he said gallantly. He was in his mid-forties, no wedding ring, fit-looking in his nice business suit, the obligatory touch of distinguished gray in his short, thick dark hair. He looked familiar, and after a moment's thought I placed him as a man I'd often seen at the pool, whizzing past with a kickboard and chatting with the best-looking women at the end of each lap. He glanced at me with interest but no recognition. I stick to the slow lanes at the pool and do my best to be completely anonymous to the men.

Vivien introduced us, a speculative look coming into her eyes. Like many women her age, she was an inveterate matchmaker, and she had long wanted the single women around her, for instance me and Delores Mitchell, to settle down. Me especially. She blamed all my problems on lack of a good man.

"This is Ted Ramsey, Liz. My dear friend Liz Sullivan, Mr. Ramsey. She teaches my writing workshop, you know."

"I didn't know." He smiled at me, but I knew I'd been dismissed as someone with nothing of value for him. Turning back to Vivien, he lowered his voice a little.

"Have you thought about our talk, Mrs. Greely?"

Vivien looked troubled. "Well, yes, I have, Mr. Ramsey. But you know, I'm just not interested in selling my house. That senior housing is very nice, you're right about that, but I've lived in my house so long now—" Her voice died away.

"I can understand," Ramsey told her, sincerity oozing out of his every pore. "Naturally, if the idea doesn't appeal to you, I wouldn't press you in any way. But if you ever change your mind, I hope you'll give me a call."

He put his card in her knobby fingers, folding them over gently and giving her hand a little squeeze. Vivien loved it. "I certainly will, Mr. Ramsey," she assured him earnestly.

"Nice meeting you, Ms. Sullivan." He granted me a smile. "Hope to see you around."

Carlotta and Delores Mitchell had been chatting, ambling slowly down the steps, but when Carlotta caught sight of Ted Ramsey she put on speed. For all her pretense of feebleness, Carlotta could be pretty nippy when she wanted to. Delores wasn't far behind.

"Oh, Mr. Ramsey!" Carlotta laid one liver-spotted hand on his arm. "So nice to see you." She glanced at Vivien. "Have you been successful with our reluctant one, here?"

Ted looked a little pained. Delores stepped into the breach.

"Vivien knows what she wants." She colored a little, and glanced apologetically at Ted. It was plain that despite the ten or twelve years he had on her, she found him attractive. "I know you have a project in mind, but—"

"There are so many good projects," Ramsey said gallantly. "Well, nice talking to you, Mrs. Greely. Mrs. Houseman."

Carlotta looked resentfully at Ramsey's retreating back, and turned the look on Vivien. "I hope," she said sadly, "that I never allow my own selfish needs to take precedence over what's best for my neighbors." She swept out and, with another apologetic glance, Delores followed.

Vivien sighed. "She is, of course." I must have looked puzzled. "Letting her own selfish—" Vivien sighed again. "I wish the Babcocks' house had never burned down. If their double lot hadn't come on the market, Mr. Ramsey would never have thought of putting condos there. Carlotta really wants to move, ever since last summer when a couple of the street people stripped the fruit off her plum trees. She's frightened of them." She exchanged a smile with me.

"She only tolerates me because I'm a woman," I admitted. "Last week she asked me if I had ever had head lice."

"Surely not." Vivien looked disapproving. "You see, Liz. You should settle down with someone like Ted Ramsey. No one would ever ask you such a question then."

"Too high a price to pay." I smiled to show I was teasing, though it wasn't far from the truth.

"He's so handsome." Vivien raised her eyebrows. "You could do worse, Liz dear. He's certainly well set-up, too. And very nice for a real estate developer."

"I've seen his name in the *Weekly*," I admitted. Ted Ramsey was always so politically correct that even in an anti-development climate he was able to get projects okayed.

"He was very persuasive when he came to see me, but I don't like the idea of selling." Vivien walked toward the doors, leaning on her cane. "And I don't really have to, either."

It wasn't any of my concern, but I hoped Vivien wouldn't let herself be talked into a home by some slick real-estate type. We came out into the sunlight. I blinked, reaching into my bag for shades. "Sure you don't want a ride home?"

"Walking's good for me," she said firmly. What she really meant was that climbing into my bus was difficult for her. I watched her make her slow way down the sidewalk, and hoped that she would get home all right.

There were no police cars around. Maybe they'd gotten tired of waiting for me. The thought of their surveillance was infinitely depressing.

I drove back toward the main library, behind which was the community garden where I had a plot. I needed the soothing presence of my garden almost more than I needed to collect the ingredients for dinner.

Mine is a sunny space in one corner of the big garden. In the late afternoon there weren't many other people around. The amount of ground each gardener gets is not huge—mine was ten feet by twenty. But I managed to get a good part of my sustenance from it.

There were still tomatoes on the vines, and peppers, and the root vegetables I'd planted in August were at their tender best. I pulled a few beets and carrots, and cut some romaine and rocket, using the garden hose to clean them.

It was pleasant in the bright air, tinged with the autumn aroma of distant smoke and the fragrance of ripe Concord grapes. I yanked out a few weeds, then cut up some potatoes and planted them with their eyes facing up. My gardening equipment is of necessity compact—just a hand fork and trowel, and my Swiss army knife. But the old man who had the plot before I'd taken it over had dug it deeply, and I found I did quite well with my meager tools. I had built a little compost bin at the back of the plot, and neighboring gardeners would often trade left-over soil amendments in exchange for cuttings of herbs or extra seedlings.

35

When I went out to the bus to put away my vegetables, a big, rusty, old Chevy Suburban was pulled up next to mine. Children seethed around it, clamoring for the privilege of carrying the rake, the hoe, the basket. They seemed like hundreds of kids, but I knew there were only three. Their mother slid out from behind the wheel and busied herself with something in the front seat.

"Corky carries the pitchfork." She spoke over her shoulder. "Sam, you take the hoe. Be careful, now. Here, Mick, you take the basket." The smallest boy had been about to howl, but was placated by his burden, almost too big for two-year-old legs. "I'll get the rake."

She turned around with what appeared to be a knapsack strapped to her front, and saw me. "Oh, hi, Liz. Nice garden day, isn't it?"

"Delightful," I said hollowly. "Here, I'll take the rake." This was Bridget Montrose, the writer who had gotten me my post as a workshop leader. Her home was nearer to the community garden downtown, but she'd switched during the summer. The plots behind the library have more space.

Bridget gave me the rake to carry and patted the knapsack. It moved under her hand, and a tiny fist shot up from it. I had known that the carrier must contain her newest baby, but it still caused me to step back a pace.

We walked in together. The little fist had a death grip on one of the carrier's straps. Bridget was still patting, murmuring motherwords softly. She is not a beauty, but has a kind of inner radiance that makes you forget that her face is too round and her nose is too long. I had known her since my arrival in Palo Alto; we had both attended a class at Foothill College on how to sell your writing. She'd only had two children then. We'd met off and on at various seminars and events, and become friends.

I leaned the rake against her bean trellis; her plot was two up from mine and across the way. "Thanks, Liz," she said, smiling at me, still patting. "Moira is not so sure she wants to garden today." She opened the carrier a little. The baby was tiny still, squirming around in its pouch, its blistered little lips puckering and suckling at nothing.

"Should you have it out like this?" I gazed in fascination at those scraps of hands, red and sloughing skin like a snake.

"It's a lovely day, and she's three weeks old," Bridget said, looking at me with her eyebrows raised. "I don't expect to get much work done, but the boys needed to do something vigorous."

That they did. Corky was giving orders importantly, which so far as I could see Sam completely ignored. Between them they were really stirring up the dirt.

The baby made some mewling noises, for all the world like a kitten with its eyes still closed. Bridget plopped down on an overturned bushel basket and extracted the baby, opening her blouse matter-of-factly. I felt it was rude to stare, but the scene had an odd appeal for me, half curiosity and half a kind of wistful pain that I didn't want to feel. I looked away abruptly.

"Bridget, didn't you get involved with the police last spring? When that awful woman died?"

She looked up from absorbed contemplation of her baby, surprised. "Why, yes." Her expression clouded. "I often think of it when I come to the garden. One of the people who died—Martin Hertshorn, remember him?—used to have a plot near mine in the downtown garden."

I filed that information away. "Listen, was it a Detective Drake you talked to? I—I need to know about him."

She gazed at me for a long minute, then turned her attention back to the baby. "Yes, I met Paul Drake. A nice man, I thought. Is he—are you—?"

"He thinks I'm a murderer," I said baldly, and then looked around to make sure the little boys weren't in earshot. Corky and Sam were wrangling over an unfortunate worm they'd dug up. Mick, who wouldn't understand much anyway, was busy taking everything out of Bridget's garden basket and laying the contents in a row on the dirt. I lowered my voice. "Somebody killed Pigpen Murphy last night and dumped him under my bus."

Bridget knew how I lived. She was one of the few regular people who could simply accept that, without probing at me for reasons and offering to help me pull myself up by my bootstraps.

"Murphy. He's one of the street people?" She looked appalled.

"He was." The baby pulled its head away abruptly, and milk spurted from Bridget's nipple. She coaxed Moira back into position. "Doesn't that hurt?"

"Not after you get used to it." Preoccupation with her baby nudged out all other feelings. She smiled at me. "Since this is the last time, I can take it."

"You having your tubes tied?"

"That doesn't always work, and believe me, I want it to work." She stroked a gentle finger along Moira's busy cheek. "Babies are darling, but never again. Emery's having a vasectomy."

Emery Montrose was one of those thin, nervous guys who is always charging ahead, always thinking about the next thing before he's quite finished with the last. Somehow I couldn't picture him willingly going under the knife, relinquishing control over a rather vital part of his body to someone else. "Well," I said blankly. "Nice for him."

Bridget's laughter gurgled out. "Not at all," she said. "Since I'm the one who had the pain of childbirth, I figure he can endure this one for me." She plucked Moira off and tucked her back into her carrier. "No chewing," she admonished in the voice women keep for babies. "Mommy doesn't allow that."

Moira looked pretty zoned to me. "I don't think she heard you."

"It's all subliminal at this stage," Bridget agreed, zipping the carrier back up. "So, does Drake seriously suspect you?"

"He looks serious as all get-out." I thought about the

way those granny glasses reflected the light. "Can't really tell what's going on in that curly head, actually."

"He can be inscrutable," Bridget assented. "Listen." Her voice turned brisk. "Park at our place tonight. That ordinance against sleeping in a parked vehicle won't apply to a guest in our driveway."

I swallowed, trying to get the words out. "Thanks," I mumbled at last. It had been easier to be cool in a room full of police than in the presence of one friendly action.

We talked over the few facts I had, while I put in a little time weeding Bridget's garden, which certainly needed it. The boys stopped wrangling and planted some radishes and peas, which was optimistic of them. We watered everything, leaving her garden looking much better. Bridget is a lovely person, nice as they come; however, she has no head for order.

The setting sun sent cold shadows away from the trees. Bridget herded her children toward the parking lot, asking me to dinner but taking my refusal gracefully. I've baby-sat her kids before. It was a deafening experience, and I felt the need of quiet just then. I promised to show up around nine.

When they'd left, I turned my compost heap, adding the stuff I saved from day to day in another plastic bucket with a lid. Then I headed for one of the picnic areas in Rinconada Park. Using my one-burner propane stove— bought with the proceeds of a sale to *Grit*—I made rice pilaf with some of the fresh vegetables, and tossed the rest into a salad. It was delicious. I cleaned up the dishes and fixed a cup of mint tea, from my own herbs. There was still a little light left. I put on the poncho against the early evening chill.

I was reading *Kai Lung's Golden Hours* and eating a Rome Beauty when Detective Drake sat down opposite me at the picnic table.

8

HE stared at me while I finished the apple—not hurrying my bites. I kept reading, and finally he plucked the book out of my hands and turned it around, looked at the title, put it aside. "Ms. Sullivan," he said.

I met his eyes.

"You're not at the Carver Arms."

"You really are a good detective, you know?" As soon as I'd said it, I remembered I was going to avoid confrontation. "I canceled the reservation."

"Considerate of you." He sounded just short of having a snit-fit. "You didn't let the department know."

"Something told me you'd find out." I looked around. "Little did I realize, when I read James Bond in my cradle, that one day I too would be shadowed."

Drake took a deep, ostentatiously patient breath. "There's no camping allowed in city parks."

"I don't plan to camp anywhere."

"Perhaps you'd be kind enough to tell me where you plan to spend the night, then?"

"When I arrive at my destination, you'll probably be among the first to know."

He turned red, perhaps with rage. "You," he said through clenched teeth, "are just barely not in jail, Ms. Sullivan. It wouldn't take much for me to decide you belong there."

I folded my hands politely on the table. "You're harassing me, Detective Drake. I'm following orders; I'm not leaving town." My hands were clenched together so tightly it took an effort to relax them. "Look, I haven't committed any crime. While you devote yourself to me, the person who killed Pigpen is somewhere around, free to repeat himself."

He ran his hands through his hair, stirring it up even further. No wonder it looked like he styled it with a Cuisinart. "So you say," he muttered. "But what evidence there is points just one place—to you."

I couldn't read his face. The sun had finally finished with the day; it was growing darker. A cold wind picked up dead magnolia leaves and sent them along the ground, scraping and rattling like bones being shaken together.

"You should do your job better, then," I said finally, uneasy under that steady scrutiny. "I don't like my taxes supporting cops too stupid to arrest the right person."

An unwilling chuckle escaped him. "God, you've got a nasty mouth on you." He came around and stared down at me. He wasn't a tall man, not much more than five-eight, but to a short person sitting down, he loomed. So I got up too, and he moved closer. He was standing right up against me. "It looks good, though."

"My mouth is nothing to do with you," I said carefully, around the uncomfortable mixture of apprehension and anticipation that his words sent through me.

"Did I say it was?" He stepped back, and I thought there was honest surprise in his expression. "Just a lame compliment, ma'am. It's not like I plan to kiss you or anything. That would be sexual harassment."

"You're damned straight," I muttered.

He didn't say anything else, just turned around and walked off. By the time I thought of a good retort, he was driving away.

It was a quarter to nine when I pulled into Bridget's driveway. I killed some time tidying up my stuff. When the relative silence signaled that the kids were in bed, I tapped on the back door.

Bridget let me into the kitchen. Emery called hello, but stayed in the living room, engulfed in an easy chair and *Dr.*

41

Dobb's Journal. He's in software publishing. The kitchen smelled of herb tea and brownies. Little Moira occupied a basket in the middle of the big round table, like some kind of animated centerpiece.

Bridget and I settled down to hash over Pigpen's murder. I had barely filled her in on the events of my day when the front door suffered a violent assault.

Grumbling, Emery heaved himself out of his chair and went to answer it. Paul Drake burst into the house, scowling like his eyebrows had been wired together.

"Where—oh, there you are," he hollered at me. Bridget and I were standing in the kitchen doorway.

"Hello, Paul. Nice to see you," Emery said. I wondered if Bridget had explained the situation to him. "Hey, the kids are asleep, okay?"

Drake mumbled something at him and stalked over to me. "So now you're going to involve Bridget in this mess," he thundered quietly.

Bridget shushed him, but too late. Moira, it turned out, didn't like angry voices when she was feeling drowsy.

"Don't be ridiculous, Paul," Bridget said. She spoke in a soothing voice while she held Moira on her shoulder, but she was glaring at him. "Liz is a friend of mine, and I don't see what business it is of yours if I invite her over."

He looked at her with a kind of baffled tenderness, and I realized that Bridget had claimed another victim. She doesn't usually recognize it when men get crushes on her, because she isn't expecting it. Other women don't expect it either. She's in her mid-thirties, about my age; in spite of four kids and a devoted husband, there's some virginally seductive quality about her that brings out men's protective instincts.

"Biddy," Paul Drake said to her, "you don't want to be mixed up in another murder investigation."

Emery had given up on *Dr. Dobb's.* "She isn't mixed up in it," he told Drake. "Liz is our friend, and she's completely trustworthy. She hasn't killed anyone. I don't like guests in my house being hassled."

Emery didn't seem too fond of Drake. He knew Bridget's effect on guys susceptible to her brand of femininity. He also knew he had nothing to worry about. But I guess he worried anyway.

Bridget sat down at the kitchen table, poured another cup of herb tea, and put Moira to her breast. "Paul, really, you've made a bad mistake if you think Liz is the one you're after." She pushed the cup toward him with a wide, friendly smile. "Sit down. Let's talk about it."

Drake dithered for a minute, but he sat down. So did Emery. We drank tea and ate brownies—all but Moira, who got hers second-hand—and discussed the events of the previous twenty-four hours. Bridget brought out three or four far-out theories about the killing. When she started pressing Drake for details of his investigation, he finally took himself off, completely forgetting to blast me anymore for involving his secret honey.

I hadn't said much, partly to keep a low profile, and partly because I was choking down stupid disappointment. Like a fool, I'd let myself nourish a little core of female satisfaction based on my last encounter with Drake. Seems a woman never really learns her lesson where men are concerned.

The rest of us sat at the table for a while more, kicking the situation around and trying to decide who would have wanted to kill Pigpen Murphy.

"He sure sounds disposable," Emery said, after I'd given them a brief sketch of Pigpen's most prominent character traits. "But who would take the trouble to do it?"

"Someone who hated street people?" Bridget let Moira's tiny fingers curl around hers. "He would look like the epitome of one, that's for sure."

"Did he get into trouble?" Emery inspected the brownies carefully, finally breaking one in half. "I don't need this," he mumbled. "Who did he hang out with, anyway?" The brownie vanished.

"He was one of the under-the-overpass crowd." I pushed the brownie plate away when Bridget passed it to me.

"There's a whole little subdivision down there. Alonso is the one I've mainly seen Pigpen with. I don't really know any of them."

Bridget was frowning. "If one of his friends did it, why put the body under your bus? Why not just leave it wherever, or put it in the bushes or something? That seems pretty premeditated to me."

"Now, Biddy," Emery said uneasily.

"Maybe," Bridget went on, unheeding, "it's someone trying to get at you, Liz. Not an enemy of Pigpen's at all, just of you." She looked at me, concerned. "Why don't you sleep on our couch tonight?"

"Now, Biddy," Emery said more firmly. "You're letting your imagination run away with you again. Liz doesn't need anything more to worry about."

I turned down the offer of the couch. But Bridget's suggestion, mixed with speculation about Drake, kept me awake in my bus, long after I'd put *Kai Lung's Golden Hours* away.

9

AT three thirty-five the next morning I was awakened by someone around my bus. Not for the first time in my vagabond life, I wondered if I should get a gun. When I finally managed to nerve myself to part the curtains, a uniformed policeman stared back at my sleep-befuddled eyes.

After that, I didn't sleep anymore.

Eventually the gray light came, and the sounds of children's scuffles from inside Bridget's house, and the thin wail of a baby. I debated going inside, but figured the chaos level wouldn't be enhanced by my presence. I stirred around, getting dressed, washing my face in cold water. The knock on the bus's sliding door took me by surprise.

It was Corky, his six-year-old face freckled and smiling, his red hair standing up in a series of magnificent cowlicks. "Mom says come and have some pancakes," he relayed, his gaze traveling around the inside of the bus. "Gee, this is great. You have your own sink and everything!"

"Just like a house," I agreed, climbing out. "After breakfast, if your mom doesn't need you, maybe you'd like to help me get things in order."

"Cool," he proclaimed, leading the way around to the back door. "But I have to go to school."

"Some time soon, then." I followed him through the kitchen door. The room was full of breakfast perfume—pancakes, coffee, the sharp, sweet aroma of fresh-squeezed oranges. Bridget turned from the stove to wave her spatula.

"Help yourself to the bathroom," she said, smiling. She wore the baby strapped to her chest like a shield. "I'm fixing you a short stack."

Emery was just coming out of the bathroom, his face preoccupied, already wearing the power clothes—tie, nice shirt, shined shoes, and all. "Morning," he mumbled. Although he'd been cordial and understanding the night before, his vibes now seemed standoffish. I didn't blame him. If he knew the police had spent a lot of time last night hanging around his house, he doubtless had second thoughts about my desirability as a driveway guest. I had them, too. Bridget was my friend—a commodity scarce and treasured—and I wasn't going to risk our friendship by sticking around. The Carver Arms couldn't be as bad as having policemen shining flashlights at you at three thirty-five A.M.

I washed again, in warm water this time, and used the toilet. The shower looked inviting, but I could wait until after my swim. My reflection in the steamy mirror above the sink was alarmingly insubstantial, as if I'd already begun fading away from real life. I plowed a few vertical furrows through the steam, to see my face behind bars. It was not a pretty sight. I cleaned the mirror with a towel and headed back to the kitchen.

Emery was at the table, inhaling pancakes and the morning newspaper. The kids, I guessed, were finished—splashing noises came from their bathroom, along with the usual shrieks and yells. Boys are noisy creatures in the morning.

Bridget gestured me toward a plate that waited by the stove, stacked with pancakes. She was on the phone, her face creased with worry. I found the syrup and joined Emery at the table. The pancakes were blissfully good, better by far than the ones at Jim's Cafe on University, where I sometimes treated myself to a hot breakfast if I'd made a good sale.

"What did the doctor say?" Bridget stretched the phone cord to get me a juice glass, pointing at the pitcher on the table. I made a mental note to scrounge up some oranges for her, from the trees no one bothers to pick around town. I know where they all are.

"You should see a doctor, Claudia." The baby squirmed on Bridget's chest, and she tapped Emery, who began unzipping and snapping until he could extricate Moira. He felt her bottom and carried her out of the kitchen. Bridget poured herself a cup of tea and one for me, still holding the phone between her ear and shoulder.

"Epsom salts are what we used to use, but if it's more than a sprain, the sooner it's taken care of, the better. How are you getting around?"

I ate steadily through my pancakes, idly listening to the one-sided conversation. It sounded like Claudia Kaplan, another one of Bridget's circle of writer friends. I'd met Claudia a few times. She was a tall, imposing woman who wrote well-researched biographies of important, though sometimes obscure, women.

"Well, get someone to help you with the roses. You can't take risks like that—you might fall again and really hurt yourself." Bridget was prone to mother everyone when they needed it, and Claudia was evidently no exception. After a final admonition, she hung up the phone and joined me at the table.

"She is so stubborn!"

"Claudia?" I poured a little more tea in my cup, and hotted up Bridget's. "What happened?"

"She tripped over a flower pot while she was carrying a bag of compost and sprained her ankle—or worse. That was yesterday, and it still hurts a lot. I'd better take her my medical book so she can see what to do, since she won't go to a doctor."

"I'll take it," I volunteered, pushing away my chair. "I'm going to do these dishes first—"

"You don't need to—"

"I'm going to," I interrupted. "And although I greatly appreciate your being so nice, Biddy, I can't come back here."

Emery came in, carrying Moira, and shot me a glance that I chose to interpret as full of relief.

Bridget protested. "Liz, you need a place to stay, and it might as well be here. You could put your sleeping bag in the living room, if you wanted—"

"No." I gathered up the rest of the plates and forced a smile at her. "Thanks so much, Biddy. I really appreciate your friendship. This is something I should work out with the police. It doesn't do you or your family any good for me to hang around, and I've got other places to go."

She argued with me the whole time I washed the dishes, without changing my mind. Emery finally told her to let me handle it my own way. He clapped me on the shoulder and went to herd the children into the car for school.

Bridget gave me the medical book and reluctantly let me leave, since the bus was blocking Emery's car. It was more than the pancakes that made me feel warm when I backed out and drove away.

47

10 _____

    I'D been to Claudia Kaplan's house once before. It was in the section of Palo Alto called Professorville, built mostly around the turn of the century when Stanford was hiring faculty from East Coast universities. The new arrivals erected rambling brown-shingle homes resembling those they'd left in the East, and filled them with children. Now those houses cost fortunes.

    Even Claudia's would have gone for a pretty penny, though the paint was flaking off its windowsills, and the shingles on the roof were ruffled like a dog's fur stroked the wrong way. There was a moon gate beside the house, overgrown with ivy, and tall somber yews guarding the front steps.

    I rang the bell, but no one answered. In fact, I couldn't even hear the bell inside—it was probably broken. Finally, clutching Bridget's medical book, I pushed open the moon gate and went down the overgrown path that led to the backyard.

    A figure was visible in the greenhouse at the rear. Between the back steps and the greenhouse door was a big garden, crammed full of stuff. I like gardens, and this one was intriguing. There were roses of every habit, climbing into trees, lifting rampant branches. Huge salvias towered over asters and chrysanthemums. Even the pot herbs were overgrown. I wondered what kind of fertilizer she used.

    Knocking on the open door of the greenhouse, I cleared my throat. "Mrs. Kaplan?"

    She turned, her royal purple housecoat swirling. Claudia

Kaplan had an imposing shape, hair the color and texture of iron, and the sharp, cold stare of a strict fourth-grade teacher. After a moment of scrutiny, she recognized me.

"Oh, yes. Liz Sullivan. What can I do for you?" She shuffled forward slowly, leaning on a cane. She wore bedroom slippers, and one ankle was swathed in an elastic bandage.

"Bridget wanted you to have this." I handed over the medical book. Claudia took it, holding it at arm's length.

"Nice of Biddy," she said dismissively, "but I know what's the matter. It's just a sprain." She winced a little, nonetheless, when she headed for the greenhouse door. "Can I offer you a cup of coffee or something?"

I remembered hearing comments about Claudia's coffee. "No thanks. I've got to be going." Following in her slow wake, I noticed the cuttings that rooted on shelves and tables, the labeled rose hips scattered about. "Are you hybridizing here?"

She looked over her shoulder, narrowing those gimlet eyes at me, and ran smack into the compost bin, banging it with her sore foot. I grabbed her arm before she toppled over. Together we lurched to the wooden bench outside the greenhouse.

"Thank you." Her mouth was folded small with pain. She took a few deep breaths.

"Maybe you should see a doctor." The medical book had slid from her hand, and I picked it up, leafing through it until I found the section on sprains. "It says here that if it's still swollen forty-eight hours after injury, see physician."

"Of course it says that," Claudia muttered. "It was written by doctors, wasn't it? I'll soak it for a while, and it'll be fine."

"Says here to use ice." I showed her the page in the book.

Her lips tightened. "Ice, warm water—I'll use them both." She looked around the garden and sighed. "As a matter of fact, I am trying to cross some roses, and this is the time to break up the hips and germinate the seeds." She looked at me consideringly. "I remember Bridget saying that you baby-sat and such. Do you do garden work, too?"

"I garden, yes, mostly for food." My community garden plot would have fit into her backyard ten or fifteen times and left room for a tennis court. There was a motley collection of outbuildings beyond the greenhouse. She must have had the biggest lot in the neighborhood.

"Would you like to help me for a few days?" Claudia sounded a little hesitant. I guessed that she didn't often ask for help of any kind. "I'd pay you, of course. And it's just till I get back on my feet."

"That's nice of you, Mrs. Kaplan—"

"Claudia, please."

"Claudia. But I don't know if I'll have time. I'm kind of involved right now in a murder investigation."

"Murder!" She swung around on the bench, aiming that fourth-grade-teacher look at me again. "Tell me," she commanded, "all about it."

I hesitated for a minute. Normally, I am not the kind of person who confides. But since I'd already told Bridget about the investigation and what the police were doing, there didn't seem to be any reason not to tell Claudia, too. It made a long story, while the sun poked through the rose vines and tree branches and finally freed itself to shine directly into our eyes.

The police interrogators had nothing on Claudia. She asked questions, and I answered them, compelled by the very enthusiasm of her inquiry. At last she was quiet, her hands folded on top of her cane and her chin resting on her hands.

I let my fingers trail idly through the asters that crowded beside the bench, their fringed blue petals and golden centers making a heap of brightness. Claudia's interest in the story had been different from Bridget's. Bridget had been distressed for me, her friend; Claudia, I could see, regarded it in an intellectual light.

"You should stay here," she said at last, briskly. "Biddy was perfectly right, as usual; I do need someone to help me

50

while my ankle is bad. I'll pay you for the time you put into the garden—just a few hours a day will be enough. I'll trade you room and board in return for you shopping and cooking—I don't cook well under the best of circumstances. And you'll have to tell me everything, mind you."

"I have," I began, bewildered by this sudden settling of my affairs.

"I mean, all the new stuff, as it happens. That Detective Drake has the brain of a codfish. Anyone can see you're not guilty. He just needs a suspect, so he fastens on you." She smiled at me with true warmth. "Actually, I've been a suspect of his in the past. It will be a pleasure to hand him the solution to his little problem long before he can come up with it."

Vagabonds have an instinct for traps. I didn't believe Claudia meant to trap me, but staying with her, shopping, going to bed in her house—I had lived a hunter-gatherer existence too long for that.

"I can't impose on you so much," I said, standing up. She struggled to rise, and I lent her a hand.

"It would be no imposition," she said, upright again. "I really need the help."

She didn't look too good, leaning on her cane like some tottery grande dame. But she was sharp. She saw my hesitation and zoomed in on it.

"Of course, if you won't help me, I might be able to find some teenager to come in." She sniffed. "I couldn't trust them in the garden, though. This year I'm hoping for a really spectacular result from crossing Oklahoma with Sheer Bliss."

I had once worked at a commercial nursery. I had even had a small rose garden, before the necessity for taking up the vagabond life came along. Oklahoma was my favorite hybrid tea—its dark beauty and fabulous scent were the epitome of rose-ness.

Through the greenhouse's open door, I could see the workbench scattered with fascinating tools. But I still argued with myself. Only a fool would fiddle with plants while murder charges swirled round her head.

But then, I've never claimed any particular degree of sagacity.

"I want to stay with my bus," I said to Claudia, finally. "But I'll park it back here by your garage. I can get the meals and help in the garden for a couple of hours in the mornings. I have commitments for the rest of the time. And the police will want to know I'm staying here; they may hang around a lot and bother you."

Claudia, her face triumphant, waved the police away with a majestic hand. "They won't bother *me*," she said, and I could believe it. "The garage is rather dilapidated but you won't mind that. And you can have the bathroom off the kitchen for yourself, if you'd like." She mentioned the money she would pay, and I told her it was too much. We argued about it all the way down the path to her back door. I didn't win. Not many do, I fancy, when they come up against Claudia.

Flushed with victory, she rested for a minute before climbing the back steps. "You should sleep in the house," she said, returning to the attack. "More comfortable for you, and less dangerous."

"Dangerous?" The conversation was totally out of my control now. Claudia began to struggle up the steps, and I boosted her a little from behind. "I've never had any problems."

"Until now." Claudia threw open the back door and invited me to enter with another one of those queenly sweeps of the hand. "Don't you see? If someone has it in for you, you're about as safe inside that van of yours as a sardine in a tin."

11 _____

I refused to sleep in the house. I began to wonder if I should even work for Claudia, and, as if she saw her prey vanishing, she stopped pressing me. She was out of breath, anyway, by the time she made it into an old over-stuffed rocking chair that was parked, higgledy-piggledy, by the kitchen door. At her request, I put the kettle on for some coffee.

The coffee she intended to drink was an enormous jar of instant, on the counter beside the stove. There were some tea bags in an old cardboard box; I don't care for Lipton, but in a pinch I'll drink it. In the refrigerator were a pint of soured milk and half a head of exhausted iceberg lettuce. The cupboard held several little tubs of Cup o' Noodles and one loaf of bread, half-eaten, with attractive blue mold spots blossoming on it.

This last Claudia regarded with interest. "I've always wondered what you have to do to bread mold to turn it into penicillin," she remarked.

"Is this all the food you have?" I looked deeper into the cupboard. There were a few crackers, some vintage Worcestershire sauce, and a jar of home-canned peaches, the top ominously domed. I threw it away.

"Haven't been to the market for a while," Claudia said vaguely. "Usually I walk downtown for lunch." She glared down at her swollen ankle.

I made a list, more hindered than helped by her suggestions, and left her with the ankle wrapped in ice and a stack of ancient diaries at her elbow that pertained to her research into the life of Juana Briones, her next biography subject. She gave me a blank check to the closest market and probably forgot about me as soon as I walked out the door.

It was still fairly early—shortly after ten. My whole routine was upset. Usually by this time I would be at the library, ready to work on research, or parked near Rinconada Park, typing up a manuscript to send out. Now, in my new role as gardener/cook/handyperson/murder suspect, I was shopping. Life is strange.

Outside the Whole Foods was a pack of newspaper machines. I never buy newspapers, but I like to scan the headlines through the machines' glass doors. The *Redwood Crier* had it on the front page, above the fold. I could see a tantalizing bit of headline—"Homeless Man in Suspicious Death"—and the lead: "Gordon Murphy, an often-seen character on downtown Palo Alto streets, was found dead early this morning by an unidentified vagrant. Murphy, 42, was—"

If I wanted to read the rest, I would have to buy the paper. I didn't want to read it, to find myself referred to as a vagrant. Vagabond is a much more attractive word choice.

It was funny to think of Pigpen as Gordon Murphy. The name dignified him, took away the macabre overtones of his death, rendered it tragedy instead of melodrama. Gordon Murphy should have had a future, a family, a purpose. Pigpen Murphy didn't even have the next bottle anymore.

I went on into the Whole Foods, trying to tamp down the apprehension that had come back in full force after seeing the newspaper. It was all real, far too real, and I was in far too deep for a person who likes to stay out of things.

The market was a good distraction, anyway. Whole Foods is like a temple to Health, with side altars to Wealth and Weirdness. I don't usually shop there—or anywhere, having discovered how to eat with a minimum amount of spending. Generally, when I want novelty in my diet, I go to Common Ground, the seed place, and pick up something for the garden. It teaches patience.

The grocery carts were as wide as Rolls-Royces. I tooled

carefully through the aisles, wondering how anyone chose which vitamins to take, which teas to use. There was an herbal cure for every disease hypochondria could conjure. They had every variety of tofu known to humanity. Strangely enough, there was a great meat counter in the back, giving the place a kind of rich, high-toned schizophrenia. The Halloween pumpkins were organic; the candy goblins and witches were made from some kind of ersatz chocolate. The bakery displayed both knobby, whole-grain health breads and brownies so sinful as to defy description.

I knew, because I sampled everything out of little baskets set at the counters. I collected some good tea, fruits that were unavailable by scrounging, vegetables that were out of season in my plot. There was a nice-looking salmon staring me in the eye, so I got some of that, too. Drunken with the power of that blank check, I reeled through the store, adding bags of granola and half-gallons of milk and even ice cream to my cart.

"Why, Liz." It was Delores Mitchell, wearing a suit of nubby, expensive fabric, with one of the inevitable bowed silk blouses peeking out the front. Her skirt was uncreased, her alligator pumps immaculate. It didn't take her quick glance at my motley garb to make me feel immediately dowdy and unclean. "I'd never expect to run into you here," she trilled, holding her shopping basket as if she was gathering flowers. Instead of blossoms, it held a carton of yogurt, a little plastic tub of deli stuff, a muffin, and a bottle of imported mineral water.

"I eat, too," I muttered. Delores had an unfortunate effect on me, which I would like to be too well-integrated to experience. I longed for the lid to come off the yogurt carton and let the purple stuff inside trickle down her perfectly groomed front. Playground emotions, I know.

"Of course you—I didn't mean to imply—" She looked flustered for a moment. I was a social challenge for Delores; she could cosset the old folks at the Senior Center and chitchat brightly with the down-and-outers at the Food Closet, where she also volunteered. There was no convenient niche for me. When I turned up at the swimming pool or Senior Center, or at an expensive and trendy grocery store, she had to readjust her ideas about people who live in cars as opposed to houses. To give her credit, she didn't just brush me off.

"I didn't see you at the pool this morning." She smiled gaily, as if we had a regular rendezvous, instead of an occasional encounter. "My eyes positively ache from that chlorine."

"They are a little red," I said solicitously. They weren't, of course. Delores had some of those excellent goggles. Her eyeballs stayed gloriously white when she swam, unlike mine.

"Are they?" She peered at her reflection in the shiny glass door of the ice-cream cooler. "Oh dear. I'm meeting someone for lunch, and I don't want to look like I stayed up all night." She patted at her hair. "Well, Ted will understand. He swims, too." I felt again that unsettling mixture of guilt for having her on, and sneaking satisfaction that she was so easy to gull. "How is your class going?" She smiled kindly at me, working from the script that all those popular people have, the one that tells them to ask about the interests of others. "I've got more of those old dears than ever in my financial planning seminar."

"I'm doing fine." Delores looked understanding; she must have noticed that my attendance was down from the first quarter I took the writing workshop. It was all right with me; the ones who stuck with me were really interested in working, and the dilettantes had dropped out. The bad angel in my left brain drove me to add, "It's you I worry about. Isn't Federated Savings being investigated by the IRS?"

Delores looked horrified. "Oh, no! It's not true at all!" She grabbed my arm. "Where did you hear that?"

"I think it was on the radio or something." She was so worried by the rumor that my good, right-brain angel wanted me to confess I'd made it up, but that would have involved tedious and uncomfortable explanations. I wanted to get back to Claudia's, have lunch and a cup of tea, maybe sample that ice cream before starting to work.

"Federated is one of the healthiest S&L's in the business," Delores assured me earnestly.

"If you say so." I made a private resolve not to have any more of these conversations with Delores, not to pull her credulous leg again. "Got to get this ice cream home."

Delores moved in the opposite direction, but I caught her questioning glance back at me as I rounded the aisle. No doubt she'd remembered that I didn't have a home.

The groceries in my cart cost more than I spent in a month for food. The bill seemed extravagant, and yet it wasn't out of the range Claudia had set. Perhaps, if I stayed at her place more than a few days, I would treat her to cuisine à la vagabond, where the flavor of the food is intensified by the effort it takes to collect it.

I was planning to call the police department, to tell Drake or Morales where they could find me for the next few days. That little task was not necessary, though. Drake was leaning against my bus when I came out of the store. His manner was idle, even proprietary. Not, this morning, threatening.

"Ms. Sullivan." He greeted me matter-of-factly, watching while I stowed the grocery bags away. "Did you rob a bank?"

"Just working for a living," I said, facing him. Delores Mitchell climbed into her BMW three cars down. She watched curiously, making a big production out of finding her sunglasses.

"Are you going to stay at Biddy's, or are you going to the Carver Arms?" Drake sounded relaxed, but his smile was tight.

"Neither." I fished a notebook out of my bag and scribbled Claudia's address on it. "I'm parking here, around the back. There's a phone, too, if you need to get in touch with me. Claudia Kaplan."

He raised his eyebrows. "Mrs. Kaplan is a friend of yours?"

"Not exactly." From his expression, he'd tangled with Claudia a time or two. "She needs help in her garden, and in the house. With luck, you'll have cleared up this whole mess before I'm finished there."

"With luck, you won't have a new address at the county's expense," he said mildly.

I didn't like to think about that. "Have you found out anything more?" I kept my notebook open, just in case he decided to shake some information loose. Delores Mitchell drove slowly past us and out of the parking lot, so intent on my conversation with Drake she almost ran over a grocery cart.

"When I find out something you need to know, I'll tell you," Drake said, smiling a little to take the sting out of his words. "But I did wonder if you could help me. We're looking for a guy who was a drinking buddy of Murphy's—Alonso Beaudray. Do you know where he can be found?"

"Alonso." I thought about it for a minute, tucking my notebook back in my bag. "I told you already, they were part of the underpass gang. Maybe they had some other place, too." It would be all over the street soon that I was being followed and questioned. "They might know. I didn't hang around with that group."

"Who did you hang around with?" He made it sound like a casual inquiry.

"Nobody." I smiled sweetly. "I'm a loner, Mr. Drake."

"But you weren't always, Ms. Sullivan. Or should I call you Mrs. Naylor?"

I thought I had prepared myself for it—the police's discovery of my unsavory past. And yet the sound of that name made my heart stop and start again in slow, uneven jerks. Through the fog that seemed to veil my eyes, I could see Drake's face, his smile changing to concern.

"It's always best, when you run away," he added lamely, into my frozen silence, "to do more than just use your maiden name. We traced you very easily." He cleared his throat and added gruffly, "Guess I know now why you hate men."

Words wouldn't come out through the dryness of my throat. I swallowed and fought my face for control.

Drake watched me, his glasses winking in the sun. "We know what happened to you," he added. "You must see that it makes you more interesting to us."

"Did you—did you tell—" This time I managed to speak. It hurt.

"We didn't interview your ex-husband." There was a flash of uncertainty behind the glasses. "He won't know where you are."

"He'll find out." I rounded the front of the bus, Drake at my heels, and climbed into the driver's seat. "He's very good at that. He'll find out."

"Look, Ms. Sullivan—Liz. I'm sorry. But you didn't come clean with us, and you should have. Then we wouldn't have had to ferret around." He shuffled his feet. "Listen, just let us know if there are problems, okay?"

"Sure." I stared down at him bitterly from the driver's seat. "I'll call you right up on my two-way wristwatch. I have to go now."

He was still standing in the parking lot when I left. I drove back to Claudia's as fast as I could, and I wasn't worried about the ice cream.

12

CLAUDIA was still sitting at the kitchen table, but she had switched to the bucket of hot water with Epsom salts. She was deep in a pile of photocopies, her elbows on either side of the stack, her face bent territorially over it.

I set two bags of groceries down with a muttered hello, and went back for the third one. My hands had started shaking again as soon as I'd let go of the steering wheel. I felt numb, as if all my synapses were paralyzed.

"What's the matter?" Claudia ceased to focus on her papers, and turned her sharp eyes on me. I avoided them as long as I could, but at last the cans and bottles were all put away, the bread stashed, the refrigerator stocked. I shut the freezer door and turned to look at her.

"Nothing." I didn't know yet what I'd tell her, how I'd get away. I needed time to think.

"Has there been another murder?"

"Not yet." I had planned a fancy salad for our lunch, but now I set out bread and sandwich fixings and let it go at that.

Claudia made herself an immense tower of cheese, tomatoes, sprouts, avocado, and lettuce—everything I'd put out. I stuck my spoon into a carton of yogurt and pretended to swallow.

"Are you a vegetarian?" Claudia's question broke the silence. "I notice there's no meat here."

"I bought salmon for dinner." Fresh fish was no longer exciting. In fact, visualizing that dead eye, that slack jaw, I felt positively queasy about the salmon.

There was something wrong with my mind. It took ordinary things, like the yogurt I was trying to eat, and used them to remind me of hideous events in the past. Yogurt was a lot like the vanilla pudding Tony had shoved my face into, the time he said I hadn't put enough sugar in it. Raw meat was what I'd seen the night he'd laid my arm open with the bread knife. He'd accused me of sneaking around with his best friend. My denial had just enraged him. The blood calmed him down some; there was quite a bit of blood.

I looked around at Claudia's kitchen—the cracked linoleum, the ancient appliances. It reminded me of the kitchens in apartments we'd rented, the backdrop for Tony's war against me, psychic damage escalating to physical violence over five long years.

But, of course, the bedroom can be a very violent place, too.

"Liz?" Claudia touched my arm. "Are you okay?"

"I'm fine." I took a deep breath. "I won't be able to stay and help you. I have to go now. Sorry about the roses—"

"The police have solved the murder?" Under her stern eye, I could not tell a lie. I shook my head.

"Then you're behaving foolishly," she went on, giving my arm a little shake before she let go. "Flight presupposes guilt, you know. Why are you so scared now? You weren't before."

It was strange that I would confide in Claudia, who had not an iota of Bridget's reassuring sympathy. But as if her question was the off/on switch to my memory, I started talking. It poured out, to the point where the sound of my voice sickened me, and yet I couldn't stop until I'd told it all.

Claudia listened without interrupting, without moving. I told her how I'd run away from college with Tony, who was so hated by my family that I'd never heard from them again. (Could I bear to admit to them how right they were?) How I'd kept us alive through a variety of jobs, while Tony went to one school after another, moving from town to town, from premed to prelaw to engineering to drafting to radio announcing school, never settling down to anything but drinking with his buddies after class and coming home afterward simmering with anger at the world, at the universe, at me—the personification of everything that held him down. I left him a couple of times, and he threatened me, frightened me, until I didn't know where to turn except back to him. Always the promises, the sweet talk—and then the doubts and suspicions that led to violence.

The last time, when he knocked me against the headboard, his eyes narrowed with that crazy glitter, I knew he would kill me. I got the nightstand drawer open before he could. I wanted him to die, wanted to die myself. I'm a lousy shot. I've never decided if that was bad or good luck.

I have a nightmare that comes again and again, about pulling that trigger, seeing him fall back as if the bullet had pushed him over, seeing that bright red delta grow and grow on his chest. In my dream there's a long, silent time between him falling back and my hand going to the telephone.

Claudia leaned forward; the creak of her chair sounded loud in the room.

"So you didn't kill him?" Her face was cold, dispassionate.

"No."

She took a deep breath. "Too bad."

I tried to smile. "Tony doesn't see it that way."

"Hmm." Claudia had already abandoned the speculative for the concrete. "I wonder how the police traced you? What address does your driver's license have?"

"An accommodation address in San Jose." I had my official mail sent there, since it was a street address and not a box number. They sent it on to my PO box in Palo Alto—for a nominal fee every year. It wouldn't take a very substantial bribe to be worth more to them than I was. "Fingerprints, probably. I was sort of hoping they wouldn't bother to check them."

"Just like in books," Claudia said. "They must have run you through some computer to see what came up."

"It just goes to show that dishonesty should be total." I got up to put away the food. "It's a lesson I'll take to heart next time around. New name, new background."

"Why didn't you do that this time?" Claudia sounded interested, as if my life was some PBS presentation—"How the Vagabonds Got That Way."

I shrugged. "It sounds stupid, but I'd been selling freelance articles in prison under my maiden name. Once I got out, I didn't want to lose momentum by starting over with a new moniker."

Claudia watched me for a minute, doodling on a sheet of

paper. "I don't think you should leave," she said, finally. She spoke calmly, as if my future was an exercise in logic and she was ready to present her side of it.

"Why?" I put the kettle on for some tea and sat down. Her detachment was contagious. Perhaps that's a by-product of shock. My decision to go or stay seemed no more weighty than the most commonplace trip to the market.

"If you leave," Claudia pointed out, writing LEAVE on her scratch paper, "the police will stop looking for Murphy's real killer—unless someone else dies. Even then, they'd pin it on you." She thought for a minute. "Unless you're in jail by then. Maybe."

"I'm not going to be locked up again." I had spent enough time paying for the crime of shooting my husband before he killed me. It could have been worse—the minimum security facility wasn't as bad as being in prison. Being there was better than being Tony's punching bag. He'd shown up several times, according to the staff, protesting his forgiveness of me and vowing eternal love, but I didn't have to see him. Some parts of paying my debt to society had been positive. But it was not an experience I wanted to repeat.

"You might not have a choice if you run and they find you," Claudia said pragmatically. "But if you stick it out, the dangers are that the police will pin the crime on you anyway, and/or that your ex-husband—is he an ex-husband?"

I nodded. My first act in the halfway house had been to research ways to divorce Tony without his cooperation. I got my probation transferred to Las Vegas and worked as a temp until the divorce went through.

"So if he finds out you're in Palo Alto, he's still got to track you down," Claudia went on. "That could be a lot easier if you're on the street than if you're here. Does he know your car?"

"I don't think so." I looked around the kitchen again. Claudia presented her four walls as safety, and I wanted to see them that way. But to me the house was a large, well-baited trap.

"So if you leave, you might avoid him. But he might not even know to be looking for you. Or he might have given up a while ago. How long has it been since—"

"I've been out for over five years." I fiddled restlessly with the salt and pepper shakers. "Two years later he found me in San Diego. I was lucky then, too—got away before he saw me."

I'd been working at a wholesale nursery in La Jolla. One day I was washing up in the rest room when I heard Tony's voice in the office beyond, asking about me. The owner's wife was at the counter, and she was too sharp an old bird to hand out employees' phone numbers or addresses. I held the doorknob so tightly I can still feel its imprint in my palm, while I listened to him wheedle her, feed her a line about parted lovers, a silly quarrel. When he finally left, I drove the bus back to my apartment, casing the street carefully before I climbed the back stairs. I took only the essentials—typewriter, clothes, what food there was, my camping gear. I let the nursery and my landlady know I was leaving, gave a regretful look at the little rose garden I'd cultivated in the courtyard, and drove away. I hadn't had a house address since then, but still I never felt safe.

Claudia took another view of it. "He's doubtless got some other poor woman to beat up now," she pointed out. "He won't be in the picture."

"There's another scenario," I said, gulping my tea despite its scalding heat.

Claudia looked at me, her eyebrows raised.

"He's already in the picture." I set my cup down, carefully, proud that my hand didn't shake. "Maybe Tony's decided I need to be punished some more, and this whole thing is his way of achieving that."

13

MY impulse was to flee, but in this case I had to recognize the force of Claudia's arguments. However, I did hide the bus. Claudia's garage was at right angles to her driveway, which extended a little way past the sagging garage doors to make extra parking space. There were six weedy feet between the garage and the old board fence that marked the rear of the property. I drove the bus back in there, where it was concealed from the street. If Tony had traced me, he knew what my transportation looked like. So I wouldn't drive it for a while.

I'd planned to go to the library and then swim, as usual. It took me a while to fix the tires on Claudia's bike, lube the chain, and tighten the brake cables. By then I knew the lap swimming time was nearly over, so I headed directly for the pool, after telling Claudia where I was going. If she heard me, it was a miracle. She was deep in her papers, a big mug of cold coffee clutched in one hand.

It wasn't very far to the pool. I handed my ticket to the guy who sits in the little office there, and headed for the women's locker room.

"Ms. Sullivan! Liz!"

I'm not used to being called by mellow male voices. I turned, to see Ted Ramsey bearing down on me. He was fully clothed, but his hair was wet. He carried a gym bag. It dripped a little.

"I thought you looked familiar from somewhere." He smiled at me, revealing white, even teeth. "Must have seen you around the pool."

"I swim often." I didn't reveal that I had noticed him at the pool. His ego, from all appearances, needed no stroking.

"So you're a friend of Vivien's. Isn't she the sweetest person?" His face clouded. "I don't like to think of old people living alone like that. My grandmother broke her hip and it was several hours before anyone found her. So painful."

"Vivien likes living alone." I looked at him coolly. "And she has tenants in the cottage to help her out."

"It's vacant now, though, did you know?" I had known, actually—Vivien had asked me if I was interested in renting it. If it hadn't been for the money, and worry about Tony finding me, I would have liked nothing better.

"She'll find someone great. She always does."

He held out a hand to stop me when I moved away. "Tell me—have you known her long? I just wondered—" He paused, and then continued, flashing those teeth at me once more. "I am very interested in acquiring that property. Mrs. Houseman, one of Mrs. Greely's neighbors, has given me an option on her property, and is anxious to have it all settled so she can move into the retirement home she's chosen. Don't you feel it really would be best for Mrs. Greely, too?" He shrugged slightly. "You know how these old ladies get. Don't know when they should give it up. Perhaps we could meet for dinner one night and I could explain it to you."

At least he didn't offer to make it worth my while. I stared back at him. "I wouldn't presume to advise Vivien on her living arrangements. If you'll excuse me, Mr. Ramsey, I don't have too much time for my swim."

"Of course." He conceded defeat gracefully, I had to give him that. His warm gaze traveled over me as if he saw something delightful. "I'm sure we'll meet again, Liz."

At least the incident had value in distracting me from the pile of troubles I was dragging around. Ramsey reeked of class. But I would also back Vivien every time. Beneath that sweetness was a solid, stubborn core. She liked her house. She didn't want to move. Ergo, Ramsey could

sweet-talk her all he wanted, and he would probably get nowhere.

After my twenty laps I stopped at the library to see if
they'd gotten the interlibrary loan I'd requested, microfilm
of the old *Mayfield Republican* for the late 1800s. It wasn't
in yet.

When I got back to Claudia's I sat in my bus typing up
the research I'd already done until I'd used up all the words
I could find. The writing seemed leaden and unappealing,
but at least I was back in my familiar surroundings, even if
the parking spot didn't have the scenic value I usually liked
in my decor. One advantage of driving your house around
is that you can change the view whenever you like. I'd had
some spectacular living paintings on my wall—the ocean
from Pillar Point, towering redwoods at Big Basin or
Butano, the whitewashed buildings of Fort Mason. When I
had the gas money, I could check out some great stuff.
That's what I liked about the Bay Area. If I had to leave,
it would be sad.

When the words were gone, there was no use chasing
them. I locked the bus, thinking about how I could get the
broken window replaced without driving it anywhere.
Claudia was still deep in her work when I went into the
kitchen for a drink of water. I envied her that concentration.
I wouldn't interrupt her to do those hybridization experi-
ments she wanted to try, but there was plenty of other
work.

I raked and weeded, clipping the most rampant ivy and
pruning away the wisteria that impeded passage from the
back to the front. I was shaping the clematis that overgrew
the moon gate when I saw Alonso shambling down the
street.

It took me a moment to figure out why the sight of him
was so unnerving. And then I realized that, like Pigpen just
before his death, Alonso wore fresh Goodwill-style clothes,
with no patina of ground-in dirt.

He went up the front walk of one house, a big sack in his
hand, and reemerged almost immediately, repeating the ac-

tion at the next house. Finally I realized that he was collecting the sample packets of breakfast cereal some other entrepreneur had hung on doorknobs up and down the street.

When he came abreast of Claudia's, I spoke to him.

"So you'll eat well for a few days, hey, Alonso?"

He jumped at the sound of my voice, closing his hands tightly over his bag. "Sully! I didn't see you there."

"This is a new scam, isn't it? Stealing samples?"

Scowling, he backed away. "I'm just gettin' rid of junk mail for these people."

"You got dressed up for it, I see."

He flushed, looking down at the shapeless plaid sport coat that flapped around his spare figure. "A guy needs some new clothes once in a while."

"They look good, too," I said. His hair was combed back from his face—you could see the furrows the comb's teeth had plowed in the greasy locks.

"Thought you were in jail." Alonso didn't meet my eyes. "Didn't they finger you for Pigpen's check-out?"

"They haven't so far." I could see this didn't reassure him. "Maybe there is justice in the justice system, hey?"

He thought this over. "Maybe," he said, sounding doubtful. "You didn't stiff him?"

"No, I didn't."

Alonso's forehead corrugated with the effort of thinking. "But—if you didn't do it, who did?"

"That's what we're all wondering right now, Alonso." I looked at him closely. "Do you know something more than you told the police?"

"No, no," he said hastily. He was lying, and I thought about calling him on it, but the code of the street is no prying, no lectures. It's anarchy—everyone governs his own conscience.

"You should tell them anything you know. The guy who talked to me—Drake—he's pretty much human."

"He's a cop, though, isn't he?" Alonso was already turning away. "I gotta go. See you, Sully."

Clutching his bag of cereal samples, he made off down

the street, the coat flapping out behind him. I'd never seen him move in such a hurry.

I fixed dinner for Claudia, though I couldn't summon an appetite. She didn't bring her work to the table, but I sensed this was a big concession on her part. We talked about our projects and I complimented her on her ability to tune out distraction.

"It really comes from living alone," she said, taking another serving of salmon. "After Alfred died, I started losing myself in work to keep the pain at bay." She shook her head. "Doesn't matter how long it is, you still miss them. These are his slippers, you know." She lifted one foot, lumpy with elastic bandage. "I never got around to getting rid of his stuff, and now I find myself raiding his closet. Another way to feel close to him still."

"How long has it been?" I pushed a few green beans around on my plate.

"Since he died?" She thought for a moment. "Close to ten years. You'd think I'd be used to it by now. Guess I am, really. But I've very much enjoyed your companionship, Liz. Better than a husband in many ways." She grinned mischievously. "You don't need help finding things all the time, for instance."

"It is nice to have someone to talk over projects with." I told her a little about my research, and she had some contributions to make. It was a novel dining experience for me, soothing and very pleasant, but strange, to share conversation and food.

After dinner Claudia went back to her diaries and notebooks. I read for a while in her living room—*The White Goddess*, which I've started many times and keep on hand to lull me into sleep. It didn't work this time. The living room was big, full of shabby furniture and dust, a totally foreign environment to me. I felt like a wild fox in a doghouse.

Finally I poked my head into Claudia's study to ask if she needed help getting to bed.

She didn't relish the interruption, and shook her head im-

69

patiently. "I can manage," she said, waving away the stairs that led to the second floor. "Going up is easier than coming down."

"I'll come in early tomorrow and see how you're doing, then." I wasn't sure exactly what my role of nurse/companion entailed. Tea and toast on a tray in the morning? Help in the bathroom? Claudia wasn't walking any better, although she'd learned to manage the cane.

"Fine, fine." It was obvious she hadn't listened to me. Her attention was fixed greedily on the heap of crumbling, ancient papers she'd collected on her desk. "Good night, Liz."

I used the bathroom that had been designated as mine. It did seem luxurious to brush my teeth in a real sink, wash my face with warm water, pee without having to squat over the bucket. I put such traitorous thoughts away. Houses were nice for ordinary people, not vagabonds.

The wind had picked up, bringing coldness with it. For the first time in a long while, the night seemed hostile. I'm used to being out in it, sitting with the door of the bus open, watching the few stars that are visible in this urban wilderness. But now I was a hunted creature, finding trouble in every shadow, menace in every gust of wind. I stood for a moment in the middle of Claudia's garden, letting the scent of the late roses calm me. It wasn't long after nine; from the houses on either side came the faint sounds of children yelling, music playing. I had always felt so safe in Palo Alto before.

Just as I got to the driveway, a car turned in, pinning me in its headlights. I was dazzled, and when the lights went out, I couldn't see. The footsteps coming toward me made hollow, deliberate sounds on the gravel.

"Waiting for me?" It was Drake. I pulled myself together and hoped my voice didn't reveal that moment of panic.

"I should have known you'd be checking up, I suppose."

He stopped a few feet away. "That's my job."

The back porch light came on, and Claudia opened the door. "You all right, Liz?" She sounded anxious.

"I'm fine." I was touched that she'd pulled herself away from her research. "It's the police, Claudia. I warned you they'd be hanging around."

She didn't try the steps down from the porch. "Is it that Detective Drake?"

Drake made a face, but when he answered, his voice was very official. "That's right, Mrs. Kaplan. Your guest is of interest to the police, you know."

Claudia's sniff was audible even where I stood. "If the truth were of interest to the police, it would be unnecessary for you to pester Liz."

Drake waited for a minute to see if she would go back inside, but she didn't. "I'm escorting Ms. Sullivan to her bus," he called finally. "Just want to make sure everything's in order."

"I'll bet." Claudia shaded her eyes with one hand. "Liz?"

"It's okay," I told her. "If he tries to drag me away, I'll scream."

She laughed and went back inside, and Drake accompanied me around the garage. "Out of sight here," he observed, pushing ahead to shine a flashlight into the bus. "That was good thinking."

"Thanks." I scowled at him. My emotions had taken a beating that day, and I didn't feel like subjecting them to yet another bout of excitement. If Drake thought he could hit on me again, he would find out his mistake.

He came closer, but didn't try anything. I was disappointed—because I had wanted to turn him down.

"What's the book?"

"I—what?"

"What's the book?" He reached out to pluck it from under my arm. "*The White Goddess*. You read the damnedest things."

"It's very soporific." I unlocked the side door and slid it open. "Instead of sleeping pills."

"Chamomile tea." He watched me step inside, made no move to follow me. "I have a cup of chamomile tea in the evening."

The dome light had come on, and I could see his face, all but the eyes, hidden behind his glasses. "That's nice," I said. "Well, nighty-night, Detective Drake. I'm going to bed now."

He opened his mouth, but I forestalled any comment by shutting the door. The dome light went out. I sat down, and he stood outside.

"When are you going to get this window fixed?" He tapped on the cardboard, and I felt even more insecure.

"When I get the money." I sighed. "Tomorrow, I guess. If there's time."

"Well, at least lock the door!" He jiggled the handle for emphasis, and I locked it, the little click loud in the darkness. He stood there for a few seconds longer, and then went away.

After his car drove off, I drew the curtains and turned on my lamp. I refused to think about Drake, about Tony, about my window being made of cardboard, or any of the events of the past two days. Instead I pulled out my sleeping bag, opened the book, and read.

I got sixty pages into it, realized that I didn't remember a thing I'd read, and turned off the light, to lie staring into the darkness, analyzing every sound in the night that surrounded my bus.

14

IT was colder the next morning, reminding me that every year, when the Indian summer warmth began to fade, I had the urge to migrate with the birds to some warmer clime. Once I actually did get as far south as Santa

Barbara, but it was inconvenient setting up the post office box, getting new library cards, scoping out the facilities all over again. I'd never gone far from the San Francisco Bay after that.

I pulled on sweatpants over long underwear, and a bulky shaker-knit sweater from a garage sale over all the upper layers. There was a shower in the bathroom Claudia had allotted to me, and I intended to use it, although I'd had a long argument with myself over letting my independence be whittled away by degrees—first a convenient toilet, then a shower whenever I wanted one; where would it all stop?

The kitchen was empty when I came out of the bathroom, tucking damp hair behind my ears. I put the kettle on and went quietly up the stairs. Claudia called to me before I reached the top.

She was still in bed, propped up on the pillows. A lump under the covers showed where her ankle was propped up, too.

"Worse this morning?" I thought she looked a bit feverish, as if she'd slept badly.

"It still hurts. A lot," she admitted. "Guess I should get an X ray."

"That's a good idea." Her bedroom was full of old furniture and stacks of books and papers. The bedside table was covered with them. "Shall I clear these away and bring you a tray?"

"That would be nice." She smiled at me with an effort. "Biddy was right after all. It's lucky for me she sent you with that book. I can't imagine trying to get around without help today."

It was my private thought that she could have had help from any number of people, and in fact Bridget did show up at the kitchen door while I was fixing Claudia's tray.

"Morning, Liz. Are you okay? How's Claudia?" Bridget carried Moira tucked against her shoulder. She looked at the tray. "So her ankle's worse, is it?"

"It pains her a bit." I poured more water through the coffee filter. "You want a cup?"

73

"Are you making tea, too? I'll have that." She sat at the table, patting Moira's tiny back. "Is she going to the doctor?"

"She says so, but I don't believe she's called yet."

"Too early," Bridget pointed out, blowing across the cup of tea I set before her. She sipped cautiously, so as not to dribble on the baby. "There're only answering services before nine."

The toast popped up, and I found some jam in the depths of one cupboard, dusty but with lid intact. "Do you think this is okay?"

Bridget held it to the light, then grinned. "It should be. I gave it to her last summer and the seal's not broken. It's nice of you to do all this, Liz."

"It's not nice at all," I mumbled, dishing up the eggs, spooning jam into a little bowl. "I'm getting free room and board, and someone to call the police for me if the worst happens."

"Oh, yes, the murder." Bridget's face grew thoughtful. "Do you think whoever it is will attack you next?"

I didn't want to go into the Tony theory. "You know me," I said instead, trying for a carefree smile. "Just the kind of woman everyone wants to attack."

Bridget got to her feet. "Here." She thrust Moira in my direction. "I'll take the tray up to Claudia. Hold her for a minute."

I held the baby, my hands nearly spanning her teeny chest, her head lolling sideways like a top-heavy flower. She opened her slits of eyes and goggled at me cross-eyed. We stood like that for a few minutes. I could sense the cry coming when she wrinkled her cheeks, so I brought her hastily to my shoulder, trying to pat as I had seen Bridget pat her, trying for that soothing murmur that seems to come so naturally to mothers.

The crying wasn't loud, but it was piercing and unsettling—the ancient defense of the newborn. I carried Moira up the stairs. Bridget was sitting on the bed while Claudia ate, but she graciously accepted her baby back.

"I'm not too good with babies," I said apologetically. The words were an understatement. I was terrified of babies, of their helplessness and mysterious ways, their complacent acceptance of total dependence.

"It's okay," Bridget said, cuddling Moira. The crying stopped. "She's really pretty good most of the time."

"She's darling," Claudia said absently. "Liz, Biddy says she'll give me a ride to the clinic. That way I won't have to impose on you."

"It's no imposition," I protested, but Claudia was firm.

"We won't get to the roses today," she said, regretfully. "At least, not until this afternoon, if then. So you just go on about your own business, whatever that may be."

"I need to shop for Vivien today—you know, Vivien Greely?"

"Oh, yes." Bridget smiled. "I'll be seeing her tomorrow. She always comes to the preschool every year with a couple of other seniors and helps us put on our Halloween party."

"The Halloween party. Of course." Last year, in a rash moment, I had promised to help at this same event. That was enough to create a tradition, and somehow I was slated to help again. Halloween parties at preschools call for a very high ratio of adults to children. I had gotten a few overnight baby-sitting jobs last year as a result of my volunteering; parents are always looking for responsible sitters who don't charge an arm and a leg.

"But, Liz." Claudia heaved herself up further on her pillows. "I thought you were going to keep your bus out of sight. How will you get to the grocery store?"

"It won't matter for such a short trip." I stacked the empty plates on the tray. "This is not that small a town, after all. I suppose I can go to the Co-op and back without attracting attention."

Claudia exchanged a look with Bridget, and I saw that they had appointed themselves the members of a select group, the Take Care of Liz Sullivan Group. "I have a car you can use," Claudia mentioned. "It's in the garage, and the battery's probably dead, but if you can get it started, I'd appreciate your driving it. I never do, and that's bad for a car, isn't it?"

"Very bad," Bridget said firmly. "Claudia would be in your debt if you got her car running again. Can you jump-start it?"

"Of course." I looked from one of them to the other. "You're very kind. I appreciate it."

"Nonsense. We're doing nothing," Claudia protested, flushing. "Now, if you'll both get out of here, I'll get dressed and we can move ahead with this day."

I had the kitchen cleaned up before Claudia needed help to come downstairs. She leaned on me and the railing, not saying much about her obviously painful foot. It was more swollen than the previous day, and I guessed it was either sprained or broken, meaning she'd have to spend some time with it elevated, instead of ignoring it as she had. I helped her into Biddy's Suburban and they drove off.

It was good being alone. Claudia had left me her keys, and I pushed her car out of the garage so I could get at it with the jumper cables. It was a ten-year-old Honda, with several dents that seemed a testimony to Claudia's absent-minded driving, but it started right up with a little coaxing. I can keep my bus running pretty well, but I don't know much about other cars, so it was a relief that it needed nothing else from me. I cleaned the dust and spider webs off its windshield and took it to one of those car washes where a fill-up buys you a session with the brushes.

Vivien always wanted the same things at the market—bread, low-fat milk, Raisin Bran, iceberg lettuce, cans of soup and tuna, a bag of apples, and a couple of packages of frozen mixed vegetables. She had a weakness for store-bought bakery goods, and I picked out a yellow cake with white frosting and some kind of red jam as filling. When I took in the groceries she would ask me to have a snack with her, and we would sit at her kitchen table, drinking tea, eating the cake, and discussing the writing life.

Her yard looked brown and weedy when I pulled up in

76

front of the little bungalow just before ten. The house was shabby, too, and I wondered how to get it painted on Vivien's limited income. I couldn't do anything about it now, with Claudia's work making extra demands on my time. But perhaps, in a month or so, when they'd caught Pigpen's murderer and life went back to normal . . . I took the grocery bags out of the car and tried very hard to believe that someday life would go back to normal.

Vivien met me at the door, her cotton housedress neat and tidy. She enjoyed having company, and we both got a kick out of discussing our work in progress. I put the groceries away, as usual over her protest, and as usual she got the tea ready over my protest. Her refrigerator wasn't as painfully bare as Claudia's, but I knew that every little dish of leftovers, every carefully hoarded scrap of meat, would be eaten.

"Thank you so much, Liz." She waved me to a seat at the table, which I took, knowing from experience that she wouldn't let me help her, though I found it difficult to watch her hobble around the kitchen. "This cake looks lovely. I'll just put some on a plate now. How's your story going for *Smithsonian*?"

I said I hadn't gotten much written lately, and she accepted it serenely. "That sometimes happens. You just have to persevere. I've been going great guns with my autobiography."

She sat down across from me and we talked about transitions and flashbacks for a while. It was peaceful, but I wanted to reestablish my routine, so after half an hour I got up to put away the cake and wash my cup.

"You don't have to do that," Vivien said, but I just smiled at her and put the rest of the cake on the covered dish where she liked to keep it. Her counter was very tidy, but cluttered also with boxes of tea bags, geranium cuttings rooting in glasses of water, a line of prescription bottles, and a couple of those samples of some kind of granola, like the ones Alonso had been collecting the day before.

She saw me looking at them and giggled. "I'm very

lucky," she said, picking one up. "Usually you just get one of these, but I got two."

"So you didn't need your Raisin Bran just yet?" I picked up Claudia's car keys.

"Oh, it won't take me long to get through those," Vivien said. "It's just fun to get something for nothing, isn't it?"

I agreed, and let Vivien usher me to the door. "I'm having my house painted, too," she mentioned, standing on the stoop. "Speaking of something for nothing. It's one of those reverse mortgages, you know? I'll get money every month on my house."

"That's wonderful." We spent a few minutes talking about colors. "By the way, I could pick you up tomorrow before the kids' big Halloween party."

"Are you going again? How nice." She turned her gentle smile on me. "We certainly had a good time last year. Of course, I always enjoy it so much. This will be my sixth time—or is it the seventh? At any rate, I would welcome a ride."

Then she went back inside and I climbed into Claudia's car, impatient for the library and the undemanding company of the microfiche reader.

15

I got exactly fifteen minutes with the microfiche before Detective Paul Drake came and hauled me out of the library.

There's some kind of heavy cultural conditioning to avoid making scenes in a library. When he materialized in front of me and jerked his head toward the door, I got up obediently. That automatic response angered me, but something in his expression had me worried, especially when he hissed that I should pack up my notes and bring all my stuff with me.

"Now what?" I demanded, when we were standing on the sidewalk outside. "Has my library card expired or something?"

He didn't reply—just looked at me. The liquidambar trees blazed orange and yellow around us; the air was a teasing combination of warmth from the sun and a cool autumn nip. Paul Drake didn't appear to notice any of it.

"Goddamn it, Liz," he said suddenly, the words practically exploding out of his mouth. "I've had a man watching Claudia Kaplan's driveway since last night, and he swore your bus was still there. What kind of game are you playing now?"

"I don't play games." I walked toward the parking lot, and he followed right at my heels, as if I were planning to dematerialize. "I drove Claudia's car. She asked me to. Had to jump-start it this morning." I glanced at him, taking in the genuine concern on his face. "If only I'd known there was a handy cop in the vicinity, I could have used his help."

"Where did you go last night?" He pushed me past Claudia's car, down to an ancient Saab a few cars away. The only visible sign of the car's function was the whip antenna. He opened the passenger door for me.

"I didn't go anywhere." The dashboard of the car bristled with equipment—dials, knobs, and other mysterious stuff. A telephone receiver looked kind of incongruous in the midst of it. "I went to bed, as you know. This morning I got up."

He clutched the steering wheel, but didn't start the car. "Then what? Tell me everything you did, no matter how insignificant."

"I got up. I took a shower. It was great. I made Claudia breakfast. Bridget took her to—"

"Bridget? You saw her this morning?" There was an odd note in his voice.

"She came by around eight-thirty, and took Claudia to the doctor. Claudia knew I wanted to keep the bus off the streets so she offered me her car. I jump-started it, then went to the grocery for Vivien."

"Who's this Vivien?"

I explained about Vivien and my weekly shopping for her. I told him how she always invited me in, and I always stayed for a while. "Then I came here. I've been here since ten-thirty or so. You can ask the reference librarian. She had to check me in for the microfiche." I glanced back at the welcome sanctuary of the library. "In fact, I didn't check out."

He ignored that. "Why didn't you just lie low this morning? Why didn't you just stay at Claudia's?"

"Because I have work to do," I said patiently. "What's all this about, anyway?"

He turned and looked at me, and then I knew. "Someone else is dead, is that it?"

"That's it." He was still looking at me. "Alonso, the guy who was Murphy's good buddy. Somebody found him under a bush this morning, close to the same place. He was stiff already."

I thought of Pigpen's open eyes, the congealed blood beneath his head, and felt sick. Fighting it, I rolled down the car window and took some deep breaths. "Was he— murdered?" My voice didn't sound right.

Drake shrugged. "We don't know yet. It might have been exposure—it was cold last night. The autopsy results haven't come back yet." He hesitated. "There were certain signs that contraindicate a natural death."

I barely heard this police-speak. "Alonso." I shook my head, wondering. "I saw him yesterday, you know."

Drake pounced on that. "You did? When? Where?"

"Hey, it was no big deal." I looked at my hands as if they belonged to a stranger. They were shaking. "It was mid-afternoon—maybe three, three-thirty. I was trimming the ivy in Claudia's front yard. Alonso came down the street, and he was acting funny—furtive, sort of. He was collecting those little sample boxes of cereal off people's front porches—had a whole bag full." I swallowed. "He had evidently been to Goodwill recently, just like Pigpen. Gave me the willies."

Drake made me go over the whole incident, from beginning to end, with a complete description of what Alonso had been wearing. I was numb now, waiting to be arrested. It was suspicious, I could see, that I would be one of the last people to see each of these men before they died.

What I didn't understand was why. Why should I be among the final visions they'd have in this mortal plane? Was there some kind of frame-up happening on a cosmic level? Or did I just have to lay eyes on a bum for him to be marked for death?

I took some more deep breaths. Drake was talking again. I'd missed something.

"—to make a statement," he said. His voice was coming from far away. It was hard to hear him over the rushing sound in my ears. "You must see—Liz! Are you all right?"

My head was down between my knees. After a moment I realized that the heavy weight on the back of it was Drake's hand, pushing me down. "Breathe deep," he instructed.

"I have been." My knees probably heard me clearly, but no one else could have. "Let me up."

Finally he took his hand away. I came up slowly. Fainting isn't at all what you might think from reading books. My heart was racing in a feeble sort of way, and I felt distinctly unwell.

"You gonna toss your cookies?"

"Cake," I muttered. "No, I'm not."

He peered at me closely. "I was going to ask you to identify him."

Cold moisture sprang into being on my forehead. I gulped more air. "If it's necessary." I tried to keep my voice even.

Drake looked at me, but didn't answer right away. He pulled the shoulder harness across me and buckled it in before starting the car. "You're really shook by all this, aren't you?"

"Of course I'm shook." I gripped my hands together, for warmth as well as to conceal their trembling. "These guys are not real assets to the world, but all the same—" I rolled the window down more. "Seems all I have to do is see them, and they keel over. It's not me, you know. I'm not murdering them, but—"

"But you wonder if someone is killing off people to make it look like you're doing it." He turned the heater on, to counteract all my fresh air, I guess. "That could be it. Seems kind of convoluted, though, don't you think?"

"It's a lot of trouble to go to." Outside the car window, streets of quiet houses went past, their gardens bright with chrysanthemums and asters. A pomegranate tree waved red globes against the sky. It was so peaceful. I felt that I stained the cleanness of the October day, that a black film wrapped me and those I touched.

"Is Claudia safe?" I had to ask. "Is Bridget?"

"I don't know." Drake didn't like to make that admission. "If we had unlimited staff, I could assign someone to watch them all the time. As it is—" he shrugged.

"Are you going to arrest me?"

"What gave you that idea?" He glanced at me. "I told you, we're just going down to make your statement. After that you're free to go."

"Why aren't you arresting me?" It came out very placidly, as if I was asking about some social matter. Drake looked uncomfortable.

"Because I don't think you did it." He turned into the parking garage beneath City Hall. "Don't tell anyone I said that, but I don't see you committing these crimes. For one thing, they have no subtlety."

"Is that so?" I felt absurdly pleased. "Thanks, I think."

"But my superiors might not agree, so why don't you try to keep a low profile?" He glared at me when he punched the elevator button. "I don't want to have to arrest you, although jail might be safer."

"Safer for me, or safer for my friends?" I muttered it to myself, but he heard me.

"That's the question, isn't it?" The elevator came, and we climbed in, standing silently facing the doors while we waited for enlightenment to come.

16

DETECTIVE Morales greeted me like an old friend. He'd arranged three big cups of cappuccino from one of the downtown espresso places on his desk, as if we were having a party. Cappuccino is not as obnoxious as most other coffee drinks, but I still couldn't manage to get any down, thinking about what was ahead.

"Liz said she'd identify the body," Drake told his partner.

Morales looked at me, worried. "Is it necessary? There must be someone else—"

"I don't mind." I grabbed a lungful of air and managed a smile.

"She can handle it," Drake said brusquely. "After I get a statement from her we'll go down to the morgue." He glanced at me. "Sorry this cuts into your writing time."

"What writing time?" I stirred my cappuccino, admiring the swirl of soft creams and tans it made. Vivien's house would look nice painted those colors. "I haven't had any writing time since Pigpen Murphy decided to die under my bus."

"He didn't decide," Morales said gently. "It was done for him. That's what this is all about."

"I know." I felt chastened, ashamed of my petulant outburst. "It isn't fair at all—to rewrite the master plan of someone's life like this. These guys may have looked like useless bums, but that doesn't make it okay to kill them." I set the cappuccino down without tasting it. "Who knows? I might be the next useless bum to get taken out."

Drake and Morales exchanged a look, and I saw that this thought was not new to them. "Well," Morales said heartily. "Let's get this statement out of the way."

They took me through what I'd done the previous evening and that morning. I was as detailed as I could be. It was impossible to help comparing this visit to the last time I graced the police station. Then I had been frightened and angry, just like now. But then my anger had been directed toward the police. Now I was coming to see them as allies. Now I wanted to cooperate. It was immensely comforting to know that Drake believed in my innocence.

All the same, I didn't enjoy regurgitating my actions to them. I like my privacy. After they'd finished writing down everything I said, they went off and conferred for a while. Then Drake took me back down the elevator to his beat-up Saab.

It took about half an hour to get to the Santa Clara County morgue in San Jose. We enlivened the journey with a heated argument over the relative merits of the Romantic poets and the Victorians. I was firmly in Browning's camp; Drake threw his weight behind Shelley. Ordinarily poetry doesn't do much for me, but it was useful as a distancing mechanism. When we'd exhausted the poets, we moved into fiction. I'm Victorian there, too. Drake tried to defend Norman Mailer, but it was an impossible task.

The morgue was located near Valley Medical in San Jose. I had nerved myself so heavily for the ordeal that its commonplace nature surprised me. First they showed me the clothes, and I agreed that they were the ones I'd seen Alonso in the day before. Then they took me into a room like an enormous walk-in refrigerator, lined with big drawer-fronts. Drake put his arm around me; I thought about shrugging it off, but it felt too warm and human across my back, his hand cupped absently around the ball of my shoulder.

The attendant drew out one of the drawers, pulled back the government-issue sheet that covered Alonso. He didn't look anything like the funeral-parlor variety of dead person. His hair was lank and matted, his skin waxy. There was stubble covering his jaw. His eyes, mercifully, were closed.

"That's him," I said. Through the strong smell of Lysol that blanketed the room, there was a hint of corruption. As soon as I noticed it, I began feeling nauseous. It wasn't Alonso so much as the thought of what lay behind those other drawers.

Drake led me out of the room, taking his arm away when we crossed the threshold. I was sorry, and then was angry with myself for being sorry. No matter how matey we became over these murders, nothing could change my true relationship with the police: they were in charge of moving me along; I would forever resist being moved. I couldn't afford to lose sight of that.

"Do you want some lunch?" We stood on the sidewalk, where I gratefully breathed in the bus exhaust and faint urine scent of your typical street in front of an urban public office.

"No." I swallowed, looking at Drake incredulously. "Do you?"

"I can always eat," he mumbled, leading the way to his car. "But never mind."

During the ride back to Palo Alto I was silent, and Drake forbore to reopen the discussion about writers. I was having a dichotomy attack of the worst kind, and it left me feeling paralyzed. Did I assist the police, grow to like them, understand them, and endanger my whole way of life—assuming that the murders were cleared up and my way of life was once again open to me? Or did I clam up, go my own way, and hope that I could keep the murderer from claiming another victim without dragging the police in?

Both points of view looked hopelessly naive. I was involved, Drake and Morales were involved, in something that had its own parameters, that took its own path, regardless of our attempts to stop it. Discovering that path might be possible for the police; it was damned near impossible for me to do alone. Others might be killed; if I didn't cooperate in the investigation, I would feel their deaths on my head.

Drake dropped me off at the library. I went in to clear up the microfiche, and didn't hear a word of the gentle lecture the reference librarian gave me. I drove to Claudia's and began bundling up the ivy I'd clipped the day before. There was great satisfaction to be found in subduing something.

17

"WE sat in the waiting room for hours, and then the doctor sent us over to radiology." Bridget spoke in a low voice, her eyes fixed worriedly on Claudia.

"What's the word?" I watched Claudia too. She was in better shape than Alonso, at least, but she was pale and obviously in pain.

"It's not broken." Claudia tried to scowl, but it wasn't up to her usual standard. "He strapped it up and told me to stay off it." She shook her head. "These pain pills make me groggy as hell. I've got to lie down."

Bridget and I helped her up the stairs. "Sorry about the roses." Her voice was raspy with fatigue. "We'll get to them tomorrow, okay?"

"Fine with me." I put a glass of water on her bedside table and followed Bridget back to the kitchen.

"What's the matter?" She set the kettle on the stove and

came over to lay one palm against my forehead in a maternal gesture. "Are you coming down with something? You don't look much better than Claudia."

"They found another dead person. Pigpen's friend, Alonso."

She sat down limply at the table. "Oh, no! Surely they don't think—"

"Evidently not. But they wanted me to make a statement and then I had to identify the body."

"Oh, Liz." Bridget reached toward me. "That must have been hard."

For just a moment, since she wanted to, I let her mother me. A hug, a pat on the shoulder—I felt my control slipping and pulled away. "It wasn't too bad," I muttered. "Where's the baby?"

"She went to sleep in her car seat and I just left her there while I helped Claudia. I'd better get her."

We sat in the kitchen, Moira making a centerpiece again, and talked the latest development over. Bridget offered to take my class at the Senior Center to spare me having to fool with it, but I wanted the distraction. That class didn't need to meet twice a week, since the ladies didn't usually do that much work. But they enjoyed any opportunity to get together and gossip under the heading of working on their writing.

"Well," said Bridget, gathering up her baby and her things, "just be careful, Liz. If whoever is murdering these people doesn't know where you've living right now, so much the better."

That sounded like sense to me. I felt like a stray dog that's so far eluded the dogcatcher and the gas chamber. Paranoia is rampant on the streets anyway, but there usually isn't such a good reason for it.

I could hear Claudia snoring from the foot of the stairs. When I checked on her, she was deep into the kind of sleep you get when you've taken medication, her mouth wide open, her body looking utterly relaxed. She would be out for hours yet.

Leaving the bus behind the garage, I drove her car. The afternoon wasn't as nice as the morning had been. There was a cold wind, strengthening every minute, and the sky was clouding over.

Vivien's house was on the way, so I swung by to see if I could give her a lift. She doesn't like trying to get in and out of my bus, but I figured Claudia's car wouldn't pose much of a problem. She was already heading down the sidewalk, leaning heavily on her footed cane.

She climbed into the car, sighing with relief. Vivien believes in keeping active, but it can be painful for someone so crippled with arthritis. "Is this a new car, Liz? It's very nice." Vivien hadn't bought a car in the past twenty-five years; though she no longer drove, she still had her 1966 Ford Fairlane in her garage. It was probably worth some money.

"A friend's car I'm borrowing." I let it go at that. No point in alarming Vivien with the tribulations of the last two days.

Carlotta came out while Vivien was tucking her skirt under her. I shut the door and waved at Carlotta, who stared short-sightedly back. It took her a moment to recognize me without my bus, I guess. Finally she waved, too, heading for her own car.

"There's Carlotta," I said unnecessarily as I started up the Honda.

"I see her." Vivien bit off the words.

"You two at outs?" I glanced sideways at her, pausing at the stop sign.

Vivien sighed. "Not really. This stupid thing is all her fault, anyway. It's none of her business whether I sell my house or not, but she's acting like I'm single-handedly keeping her from moving into that retirement place." She snorted. "Let her sell her house any old time. It doesn't have to be to Ted Ramsey. I'm not about to sacrifice my home so she can live it up in one of those places."

"That sounds reasonable." I drove around the corner, past a couple of guys survey.

Vivien craned her neck, making little tsking noises. "Dear me, so soon?"

"What's soon?" There was a gaggle of children crossing the street, shepherded by two harried young women. I waited at the stop sign while they took their time getting to the other side. "Are they tearing something down back there?"

Vivien was still looking over her shoulder. "They probably will, I guess. That's Eunice's house, you know. Not a week since she died, and already the surveyors are there. I always liked her little house, but people don't seem to want little old houses anymore. They tear them down without thinking twice." She pulled a handkerchief out of her worn patent-leather handbag. "Eunice was such a nice person. She always said there'd be no one to mourn when she passed on, her having no children. I've thought of that so often since her death. I've no children living either."

"Well, you're mourning her," I pointed out.

"Of course." She sniffed into her hanky. "No one ever had a nicer back-fence neighbor. Our backyards intersect, you know. And Carlotta's house is like the missing puzzle piece. I bet Ted Ramsey called those surveyors out to Eunice's. He's probably got a—what do you call it?—an option on her place." She shook her head. "He's such a nice boy. But he just doesn't understand how I feel about my house."

I murmured an assent, zipping into a parking place that miraculously opened up in front of the Senior Center. I could see Delores Mitchell in my rearview mirror, her BMW reflecting the weak light with a well-polished glitter. She didn't look too pleased at losing out on the space; in fact, it wasn't difficult to read her lips on the subject, even in the mirror.

By the time I helped Vivien out of the car, Delores had found a place to park. She came briskly up the sidewalk, a symphony in teal and silver-gray. "Liz," she exclaimed. "I didn't know you in a different car. Is your van in the shop? How can you get along without it?" She smiled at Vivien.

"I always think of Liz as being like a turtle, carrying her house with her. So adventurous."

A line from a Janis Joplin song flashed into my head. Janis had sung about being a turtle, hiding inside a hard shell, but ended with a defiant pledge to take good care of herself, knowing the world as she did. She hadn't really managed it, though. I hoped I could do a better job.

Delores was all graciousness as she patted Vivien's shoulder. "So nice to see you, Mrs. Greely. When are the painters coming?"

Vivien beamed. "Soon, Delores. It's like a dream come true, to have that money on hand." Her eyes clouded over. "Did you know they're already surveying at Eunice's house? Do you think it's that nice Ted Ramsey's idea?"

"Maybe they're just getting the property lines straight," Delores said, her forehead wrinkling. "There'll be a probate sale, I suppose. Who knows who'll buy that darling house? Maybe someone who wants to fix it up."

Vivien didn't look convinced. She changed the subject. "Your briefcase looks so heavy, Delores. I worry about you carrying it around all the time."

"It's actually my portable computer." Delores flourished the neat black case. "I wanted to show my group some spreadsheets today." She glanced at me, including me in the conversation. "That's what you need, Liz. A portable computer to use in your van."

And plug into my private power plant, I thought (but didn't say). "My typewriter works fine for a low-tech person like me," I said instead.

"Yes, indeed," Vivien chimed in. "Typing is a dying art now, I suppose, with everyone keyboarding. Liz can type so well she could submit her rough drafts as final copy."

"That's quite an accomplishment." Delores glanced at her watch. I thought perhaps she was being ironical, but she probably didn't have enough sense of humor for irony. "I'll be late for my class if I don't get going."

She sprinted past us up the stairs with a cheery good-bye. Vivien stared after her admiringly. "She always looks so pretty, doesn't she, Liz? And no husband! I wonder when she'll settle down."

It was a topic that held no interest for me, so I changed the subject to writing as we went slowly through the lobby in Delores's wake. The horrors of the morning began to recede, and I was glad I hadn't let Bridget fill in for me. The company of six elderly, opinionated ladies was not exactly soothing, but it provided an excellent distraction from murder.

18

I went to my garden after the class ended. It's my usual routine, and I couldn't stop it just because I suddenly had access to supermarkets. The garden had been my main source of food for the past couple of years.

The peppers were drooping. I gave them and the tomatoes a good drink, and picked a few to take back to Claudia's. I had lettuce, too, and some late beans. Normally I would have been figuring out what I could cook with my little harvest. Instead I was trying not to think about Alonso's face, slack-jawed and bluish, the stubble on his flaccid skin, the unpleasant smell that no amount of disinfectant could disguise, the extremely dead look of him.

I didn't want to be dead, too. I didn't want to occupy the next drawer in the morgue.

While I pulled weeds and mulched and cultivated and planted peas, the same futile thoughts chased themselves around in my head. Whoever was doing this killing had it in for street people. Though I didn't consider myself exactly a street person, I was well aware that I might be perceived that way. Ergo, there was danger for anyone living on the streets. And, though it might not be rational, I felt there was extra danger for me, that the killer was pointing at me.

It was almost a relief to think about Tony, to try and place him in the scene. Was he at the bottom of it all? I wouldn't put any kind of vicious craziness past him, but I had to admit that the Tony I'd tried to kill eight years ago was more likely to go one-on-one with his plans for me. I couldn't see him working through the agency of these other murders. I could only see him coming straight for me, using his own two hands.

A cold gust of wind carried away the empty little bag that had held sugar snap peas for planting. Shivering, I moved the hose over to the artichokes and began to collect my equipment. The sounds of cars driving by on Embarcadero, people coming and going from the library and community center, were muted by the wall of trees and hedges that enclosed the community gardens. The vast silence of growing things pushed out man-made noises. When several gardeners are present, the place hums with conversation and activity. On this chilly late October afternoon, there was no one around but me.

I told myself it was ridiculous to think anything could happen in daylight, in shouting distance of the library. But all the same I hurried while repacking my garden basket.

When the shadow fell across the planting bed, I wouldn't look up. I wanted to think I was imagining it, that it was a product of too much angst, too much nerviness. But I could feel eyes watching me, the vibrations of someone nearby. None of my fellow gardeners would stand there without saying anything—there would be comments about the size of my peppers, at the least.

My fingers tightened around the trowel. I turned. Paul Drake stood behind me.

"Damn it!" I jumped to my feet. "You're always sneaking up on me. Why didn't you say something? I might have duked you before I checked you out."

"You're frightened." He sounded surprised. "Sorry, Liz. I thought you heard me coming." He looked around, interested. "I've never been here before. Do you have to pay?"

The tension leaked out of me till I felt like an air mattress at three A.M. "It's a token amount." I picked up my basket. "Were you looking for me or just trying to find something to do?"

His eyes narrowed. "I'm keeping an eye on you, Liz. Everyone seems to agree that it's a good idea."

"You mean, because I may be killing people?" I shook my head. A couple of sleep-deprived nights were starting to catch up with me. "Don't worry, I'm not planning to knock anyone off in the next couple of hours. You can have dinner in peace, maybe even take in a movie."

He didn't smile. "That's like joking about terrorists in an airport."

"Sorry." I pushed past him. "My sense of humor has been impaired."

"Mine, too." He put one hand on my arm when I would have walked away. "What have you got, anyway?" I stared at him blankly, but he wasn't even looking at me. "Lettuce, scallions, beans, tomatoes—looks good."

"Everything tastes better when you grow it yourself." I shrugged. "I always think so, anyway. Ton—I've been told it's just my imagination."

"Your ex-husband told you that?" His expression didn't change, but something came and went in his eyes. He fell into step behind me down the narrow path to the gate. "Have you always gardened, then?"

"Sort of." I pushed the gate open and waited for him so I could latch it shut—it keeps the neighboring dogs out. He latched it himself, so naturally that I wondered if he'd been lying about never having been there before. "My mother always had a vegetable garden. I took it up after leaving school—helps on the food bills."

"I bet." He eyed my produce hungrily. "That stuff would run you quite a tab at Whole Foods."

"Somehow I picture you hanging out at the bakery, not the produce."

He managed to look affronted. "Someone's been gossiping," he grumbled, stopping beside Claudia's car. "Was it Bruno?"

"Detective Morales? I hardly know him." I unlocked the trunk and put my basket there, next to the portfolio where I kept the notebook for the writing workshop. It bothered me to have my stuff sitting out in the car, exposed to public view. I was too used to carrying everything around with me, neatly put away. It gave me a dislocated feeling to walk out to a parking lot and not see my bus, my home, waiting for me.

"So, I've been hinting for a dinner invitation." Drake leaned against Claudia's car as if he had all evening. "You're not picking up on it."

"Such subtlety," I murmured, unlocking the driver's side. "I'm fixing dinner for Claudia, Drake."

That gave him pause for a minute. "She doesn't like me." His voice was almost plaintive.

"She doesn't think much of you," I agreed.

"But she wouldn't grudge me a good dinner, I'm sure." He smiled at me ingratiatingly.

I hesitated. "You can't expect me to invite you to dinner. It's not my house."

"That's okay." He patted me on the shoulder. "I'm inviting myself. Police business—keeping an eye on a material witness."

"But—"

"I'll do the dishes," he said, with the air of one making a great concession.

I didn't want to like the guy, but it was hard not to. "Okay. You're on." I slid into the car and rolled the window down. "Don't blame me if you end up with your self-esteem in tatters."

"Oh, I won't blame you—for that." He walked away to his battered Saab.

All the way back to Claudia's, while I drove with the exemplary road manners that are induced by having the police close behind, I wondered just what he would find to blame me for.

19

CLAUDIA was awake. I could hear her thrashing around upstairs, and I paused just to put down the basket of veggies before I raced up to her. She was sitting on the edge of her bed, trying to pull a caftan over her head. Her eyes stared out at me from the tangle of fabric, dilated and groggy-looking.

"Let me help you." I found the armhole that had eluded her. "You should have waited until I got back."

"I'm not in the habit of waiting around for help," she grumbled. "I can look after myself."

"That makes two of us," I agreed.

She thrust herself up from the bed, tottering on one foot. "Don't start drawing a lot of silly parallels between my situation and yours," she snapped. "I want out of this bed. I want to go downstairs and look at my notes. I want a cup of coffee."

"Yes'm. Right away."

That pulled a reluctant smile from her. "Sorry to be in such a bad mood," she muttered. "I'm a rotten patient. It really bugs me to need help."

"Me, too."

She shot me a look from which the grogginess had dissipated. "I warned you, Liz. There's no comparison between having a bum ankle and being stalked by murderers." She shook her head impatiently. "God, my head feels like

95

someone performed liposuction on the gray matter. Did I hear you tell Biddy that another man had been killed?"

"That's right." Her cane had fallen out of reach; I handed it to her. "If this doesn't work, try leaning on me. Yes, there was another murder. They asked me to identify the body, lacking anyone else to do it."

"Oh, Liz." She lost a little of her belligerent air. "Do they suspect you?"

"It seems not." We moved out into the hall, she leaning on the cane, me ready to assist. Our procession stopped at the head of the stairs. Claudia looked at them for a stony minute, and then lowered herself until she was sitting on the topmost one.

"I used to enjoy this as a child," she remarked. "We called it bumping."

"Claudia—"

"Works when you're hiking a steep trail, too," She scooted down to the half-landing and made the turn.

Paul Drake stood at the foot of the steps. His face was carefully expressionless.

Claudia gave me an accusing stare over her shoulder. "You didn't tell me he was here."

"I didn't get a chance." I waited, wondering if Claudia would annihilate Drake with a few well-chosen words before throwing him out, or just boot him without stopping to talk.

She did neither. "Well, Detective Drake," she said graciously, bumping her way down the rest of the stairs, "you can give me a hand up. After all, that's supposed to be the police function, right?"

"Right you are, Mrs. Kaplan." He offered her his hand, and managed not to wince when she put her full weight on it pulling herself up.

"He wants to join us for dinner, if that's all right with you, Claudia."

She scowled for a moment, then shrugged. "Why, certainly, Liz. It's our duty to offer aid and comfort to the minions of the law." She turned to Drake. "I guess you miss Signe's cooking."

"I missed Signe, for a while." Paul Drake glanced from her to me. "She moved several months ago, and I'm still alive." His smile was tight. "Mrs. Kaplan seems to have heard the same gossip you have—that I'm ruled by my stomach. Well, no point in denying it. Can I help you fix the vegetables?"

He was handy in the kitchen, I'll say that for him. I enjoyed it myself, having had just the bus's tiny galley or the closest picnic table as a kitchen for the past few years. We worked together while Claudia watched from a seat at the table, sipping the coffee she'd demanded and making sarcastic comments on Drake's domesticity. I wondered about this Signe person—the name had a familiar sound, and after a while my subconscious connected her as a friend of Bridget's who used to come to the local writers' meetings.

"Get the man an apron, Liz," Claudia commanded. Drake was rather splashily scrubbing beets. "He's getting water everywhere. Is that why Signe left, Detective Drake?"

"She got a different job," he said, keeping his eyes fixed on the beets.

"That's right. *Los Angeles Times*, wasn't it?" Claudia turned to me. "Signe Harrison used to write for the *Redwood Crier*. I understand her new job is much more lucrative. Do you correspond?" This was jabbed at Drake, who managed to roll with it.

"She sends me scenic postcards," he replied, cutting the tops off the beets much too closely. "Like she does the other friends she left behind."

I gathered up the beet greens to stem and wash. "We're not going to eat those repulsive things, are we?" Claudia dropped the subject of Drake's former love, which was fine with me.

"They're delicious, and good for you, too." I shoved the beet greens into a pot and added a little water. Drake didn't look too enthusiastic, either.

"Where's the meat in this meal?" Claudia transferred her

97

glare to me. "I'm no vegetarian, Liz. I need red meat to keep up my strength."

"Relax." I pulled a bloody London Broil out of the refrigerator. "I picked this up especially for you this morning, when I got Vivien's groceries."

Claudia's eyes lit with pleasure. "I'd better cook it. You vegetable-lovers don't know what to do with a good steak."

"I'm an economic vegetarian," I said mildly. "Meat is hard to grow in a garden, so I only eat it for special occasions."

"I'll cook it," Drake offered.

Claudia enjoyed bossing him around—"That heavy cast-iron skillet, Detective Drake, since we don't have time to grill it. Lots of salt, mind. No, get it really hot!" Drake stood it pretty good-humoredly, and maybe he really preferred having Claudia hector him to eating a solitary dinner in his trailer. I don't mind solitude, but it was pleasant to share the kitchen with other people, to join a conversation whenever I felt like it, to set a table with china and glassware, instead of eating out of the pot that fits my one-burner stove.

The steak filled the kitchen with its aroma, and I was ravenously hungry all of a sudden. I had the veggies steaming gently, the beet greens cooked and chopped. I wanted to add a little good vinegar to them, but Claudia didn't have any.

"Bridget gave me some—it's in the bus." I took a bottle of wine out of the cupboard where Claudia had told me to find it, and set it on the counter. "Open that, Drake, while I go get it."

"Open that, Drake," he mimicked, looking through the silverware drawer for a corkscrew. "I can see this dinner was a mistake. You're losing all respect for my authority."

"I never had any to lose." I felt quite witty, going out the back door while they laughed inside. Night lay over the garden like the spangled velvet I had once fingered at the fabric store downtown. The scents of roses and jasmine were shamelessly cohabiting. The air was cold and, despite the flower scents, definitely on the cusp of a seasonal change. I picked my way through bars of moonlight, around the corner of the garage.

The side door on my bus was open. The dome light was off.

I didn't even think that Tony might be in there with a knife, or that the murderer was waiting for me. A surge of territorial adrenaline took over my thought process. My home, my few precious things, were under attack.

I launched myself through the gaping door. After the brightness of the moonlight, it was as dark as a cave in there. Crouched on the floor beside the cooler, I had time to realize what a stupid move I was making. The correct thing to do would have been to yell for the police, since one of them was right in the kitchen.

Before I could rectify my mistake, something moved in the back of the bus. It came toward the door, a dark, indistinct shape. Reflexively I grabbed at it as it rushed by, and found myself with a handful of what felt like sweatpants. The intruder fell heavily in the doorway of the bus, and I lost my grip.

The intruder straightened. An arm came up, silhouetted in the open doorway. I couldn't tell exactly what it was holding, but some intuitive part of my brain suggested that it would be heavy and would hurt a lot when it encountered my head. As the arm came down, I managed to roll sideways. Even glancing off my head, the blow had an impact like collision with an asteroid belt.

I didn't really lose consciousness. It was there, somewhere, just out of my grasp. In the dark bus there was a considering silence, and I knew as well as if it were spoken that my assailant was still there, wondering how badly I was hurt, whether to finish me off.

Then the back porch light came on, making a nimbus over the garage roof, and Drake's voice called, "Where's that vinegar?"

The looming shape at the door of the bus vanished. Footsteps raced down the driveway, crunching in the gravel. More footsteps came pounding toward the bus.

I lay there, letting the blackness of the ceiling slowly dissolve as my eyes got used to the dark. I couldn't seem to move or make a sound, although I could hear acutely Drake's muffled curse when he tripped over a loose paving stone in the path.

"Liz! Are you back here?" His footsteps stopped when he saw the open door of the bus. For a few moments there was silence, and then he was leaning over me.

I wanted very much to see his expression, but it was too dark. His fingers touched my neck, feeling for a pulse, then he moved my head gently. At last I could summon my voice. "I'm okay."

"I'll get an ambulance."

"No!" This threat brought me fully alert. "I'm fine, really." I sat up, unable to keep from wincing. "Nothing an ice pack won't cure."

Drake turned on the dome light. Even its dim radiance hurt my eyes. He felt around my head, his other hand warm and wonderfully steadying on my shoulder. "You've got one hell of a goose egg here, lady. What were you hit with?"

"Something heavy." I felt the lump myself. It was big, as he'd said, just behind my right ear. He squeezed past me where I huddled between the front seats and the pull-down table. I missed the warmth of his hand. "Round and limp-looking, it was. But it didn't feel limp."

"Rock in a sock," he said, holding up his find. It was a black dress sock, bulging horribly at the toe end. "Not the kind of weapon that's easy to trace." His eyes traveled around the inside of the bus. I looked, too. I'd left my sleeping bag out to air the night before, and it was rumpled, as if someone had crouched back between the cupboards that flanked the bed.

"This yours?" Drake was holding a little halogen flashlight, the kind with an anodized aluminum case that I had seen at Redwood Trading Post but never felt rich enough to buy.

"Nope." I reached for it, and he held it back. I noticed then that he'd picked it up with a Kleenex. "Hey, just like the real Paul Drake, but he always had a nice white handkerchief."

"I keep waiting for the generation that hasn't read Erle Stanley Gardner," he grumbled. "Did you notice if the guy wore gloves?"

I pictured again that raised arm, the strange-looking weapon, and shook my head. "Couldn't say."

He used the flashlight anyway, clicking it on with the tissue between his finger and the switch, and then shining it in my eyes.

"No sign of concussion." He switched the flashlight off and put it, wrapped, in his pocket. "Can you walk? Mrs. Kaplan will be worried by now."

"I can walk." I felt shaky, but not from being bonked. It was disturbing to think that a hostile person had been in my bus, waiting for me. "How did he get in?"

Drake's scowl was plainly visible in the moonlight. "Just cut a neat little hole in your cardboard, here, and reached in to unlock the door. Why didn't you have that window replaced, Liz?"

The window that Pigpen had punched out. I shivered. "Just didn't get around to it. My life has been rather full lately. I'll see to it soon."

"You won't sleep in this thing another night until you do." He was angry, I could tell. "Mrs. Kaplan's offering you a real room in a real house. Why don't you take her up on it?"

I wanted to be angry also. Anger is such a purifying emotion. But all I could think about was a cup of mint tea and a session with my sleeping bag. "This is real, too," I mumbled, glancing around my bus. "People who live in houses, or trailers, or apartments, don't have a lock on reality, you know."

He didn't say anything more.

I scooted forward, and remembered the vinegar as I passed my cooler, which is where I keep most food staples. The vinegar and soy sauce stand with other bottles in a little plastic tub that keeps them upright while I'm driving.

The tub had been moved.

"Forget the vinegar," Drake said impatiently. "If you don't want an ambulance, I'm taking you to the emergency room."

"Someone's been in here." I stared into the cooler. "Why would anyone break into my van to give me food?"

Drake was interested. "Good question," he said, squatting down to see for himself. "Not a real philanthropist, since he hit you on the head. What's different?"

"Things are moved around." I took out the bottle of balsamic vinegar and handed it to Drake, who tucked it absently into his hip pocket. "I can't really tell—what's this?"

Drake stared at the plastic bag I pulled out. "Looks like some kind of seed or grain," he said, puzzled. "I can see planting crack or grass to incriminate someone, but I never heard of planting granola."

20

AN ice pack kept the pain in my head from exploding outward like the fireworks that cartoonists draw around those who've been wounded. I ate a little of the steak and felt better. Claudia ate, too, and Drake polished off what was left, bit by bit, making frequent forays outside, where a couple of uniforms were spending a fun evening scrutinizing every inch of gravel in the driveway.

Claudia poured herself another glass of wine—Drake

wouldn't let me have any, and he'd stuck to mineral water. After his last trip outside, he'd cleared away the dishes. Now the middle of the table was given over to Exhibits A and B, the rock-in-the-sock and the plastic bag with its mysterious contents. I couldn't figure out if those contents looked more like caraway seeds or wild rice.

Drake had carried the bag in, using Claudia's tongs. When she reached out, he slapped her hand gently away. "Don't touch," he admonished.

"I just don't get it. Knock Liz over the head and leave this stuff behind? Doesn't make sense."

"Sure doesn't." I felt the lump again—my fingers just couldn't stay away from it. I've been beaten up worse. Once in prison I was even kayoed while trying to break up a fight between two strong, belligerent women. But it was kind of like that childbirth pain you hear women talking about—the intensity gets lost in memory, and you don't realize how much it hurts to be hurt until you're hurt again.

I could hear the sound of the bus door being slammed by Drake's colleagues, who he had explained were fingerprinting everything the intruder might have touched. "I hope they're neater this time," I said, glowering at Drake, remembering the mess I'd had to clean up a few short days before. "What are they looking for, anyway?"

"Anything that wasn't there the last time," he said absently, still staring at the bag. "For instance, you were clean before. This time, if there's drugs, there's a good chance they were planted. You want us to find anything of that nature now, when it's attended by suspicious circumstances. Not later, when someone tips us to search you."

I clapped the ice pack on my head again and felt like Alice, falling down the rabbit hole. Except that I lacked her sense of detachment. There was malice here, directed at me. I felt helpless against it, which made me angry, which made my head hurt.

Bruno Morales came to the door. I was acutely embarrassed to bring all this negative attention on Claudia's house, but she seemed to be enjoying it. "Detective Morales," she said graciously, gesturing to the empty chair at the table. "Please, have some coffee. Tell us your discoveries."

Bruno looked at Drake. "A party, Paolo?" He came closer and scrutinized the exhibits. "Strange party decorations."

"That's the weapon. What do you think?" They exchanged a long look, and I was reminded of Bridget and Emery, who have been married long enough to communicate in the same way.

"Could be." Bruno picked up the sock with its obscene burden. "Have to let the coroner take a look. Impossible to trace, eh?" He shook the sock gently by its toe, and a rounded stone dropped out. There are hundreds of thousands just like it in the deep bed of San Francisquito Creek.

"The coroner?" Claudia leaned forward in her chair. "So you think this might be how Pigpen Murphy was killed?"

I looked at her with respect. It hadn't even occurred to me to link my cracked skull with Murphy's—maybe because his had been fatal.

"Oh, no." Bruno pulled his gaze away from the bag of seeds or grains and answered Claudia courteously. "That crack on the skull might have killed Murphy in time, and it was probably administered in the same way. But what actually killed Murphy was some kind of poison, Mrs. Kaplan." He looked at Drake, again with that silent communication. "The report came in just after you left today, Paolo."

"What kind of poison?" Claudia's eyes were bright with interest, but I had caught something in that look. The tension level in the air went up several notches.

"We're not sure just now," Bruno answered easily. "But we wondered if you'd mind us taking a look around in your greenhouse."

Claudia was, for one moment, bereft of speech. "You can't be serious," I shrieked, making up for it, and setting off those fireworks again. "How in the world could Claudia have anything to do with this? She didn't even come into it until after Pigpen was killed. She didn't know him, she didn't have anything to do with him—"

"That's true," Morales said, gazing at me sadly. "But you did, Ms. Sullivan. And you know Mrs. Kaplan."

I couldn't help looking at Drake, to see how he took my return to the suspect list. He had his poker face on, but I thought I detected a bit of discomfort behind those light-reflecting glasses.

Claudia had her tongue back. "It's true that Liz and I have known each other, or known of each other, for a couple of years. But it would have surprised me greatly to find her in my greenhouse before my predicament and hers brought us, of necessity, together."

"Nicely put," Drake said briskly. "In this case, Mrs. Kaplan, such searches are more of a ruling out than anything else. We don't actually expect to find the poison that killed Pigpen in your greenhouse. But we do need to take samples of anything toxic that's there, for the lab to look at." He looked at me, and for one instant I felt his sympathy. "It's just possible, I suppose, that Ms. Sullivan could have staged the attack on herself. In order to rule that out to the satisfaction of the DA, we need to investigate it."

"I can understand that," I said hollowly. "Perhaps the DA would like to try hitting himself over the head. I can think of better ways to divert suspicion from myself."

Bruno Morales came closer, peering at my head and pursing his lips in sympathy. "You should be seen by a doctor," he said, touching the lump on my head lightly. "Not just for medical reasons, but to have the damage assessed for our reports."

"Right." Paul Drake strode toward me. "I'll take her to the emergency room now. Bruno, will you call in for me?"

I don't like doctors, or hospitals, or being bullied by the police. But there was a quality of relief in letting Drake pull me up from my chair and hustle me toward the door. We were almost out of the kitchen when he spoke over his shoulder.

"Oh, and Bruno—that sack of seeds or whatever. Take it

105

in as evidence." He pushed the door open for me, and exchanged one more of those looks with Detective Morales. "And be sure to give the lab a sample of them."

I caught a last glimpse of the kitchen before we left. Claudia and Bruno both were staring thoughtfully at that innocent, sinister bag, given pride of place on the kitchen table.

21

THE emergency room at the Stanford Hospital is busy, but not like those stereotyped places where you slowly die while waiting for help. Maybe it was just Drake's presence, but I was in a little cubicle within minutes of arriving, despite not having any blood pouring out all over the squeaky-clean floor.

The white-coated person who examined me—Dr. Kavanaugh, her nameplate said—was cheerful, joking with Drake. Me, she saw only as the busted head in cubicle three. Hospitals depress me. So many people trapped there, against their will.

I had a flashlight shone in my eyes. Dr. Kavanaugh attached electrodes to various parts of my skin while machines beeped and chattered. My temperature was taken, my pulse was taken, my knees and elbows were hit with a little hammer.

"She seems fine," Dr. Kavanaugh said finally. "We could do a CAT scan if you're really worried." She was looking at Drake when she said it. I had ceased to exist, since he'd authorized payment.

"Why don't you just unscrew my head and stick it in

there?" My words came out with a bitterness I hadn't really intended. Dr. Kavanaugh looked as if the organ grinder's monkey had just spoken, and Drake managed a fleeting smile.

"Okay, Liz. No more tests. Apparently you'll live."

"Just a bump, really," Dr. Kavanaugh agreed, abandoning the high-tech approach when it was evident no one would spring for it. "The scalp's abraded but the skin's not really broken, and the skull is unaffected." She rapped her knuckles against my head, not as gently as she evidently thought. "Hard as a rock," she said, still with her cheery smile. "You're lucky your skull is so thick."

My knuckles ached to respond in kind, but I knew the rules of institutional behavior: Don't make waves. Don't draw attention to yourself. Above all, no sassing back the keepers. Dr. Kavanaugh didn't really look anything like the attendant who'd had morning duty on my floor during my incarceration. But they had in common that ferocious jollity that is meant to put people in their place. Obligingly, I shrank back into mine.

Dr. Kavanaugh was scribbling on a prescription block. "A sedative," she said brightly. "You can get a few of them at the desk out there. In case she has trouble sleeping." I reached for the prescription, forcing my hand past the Guardol shield in which she'd enveloped me. After a barely perceptible pause, she gave it to me. With a last beaming smile at Drake, she left.

The hard, bright lights hurt my eyes. The periodic wail of ambulance sirens hurt my ears. I wanted to leave.

"Next time get your own head cracked open," I said ungraciously, sliding off the examining table. "She likes you better anyway." Those black spots were back, floating in front of my head. I reached for the table edge to steady myself. Drake put an arm around me—friendly, impersonal, like he'd do for any suspicious dame.

"Take it slow, now." He helped me out of the cubicle, pushing aside the curtain that had surrounded it. "You're not in any rush."

I stopped in the doorway, trying to breathe slowly and deeply. In the next cubicle there was a lot of groaning, punctuated by little metallic pings. "Sounds like they're digging out shotgun pellets," Drake muttered into my ear. Through a crack in the curtain I could see the metal basin with its still life of small, glistening reddish balls. A gloved hand holding some shiny tweezers appeared, and another little ball dropped into the dish.

I headed for the exit as fast as I could, pausing impatiently while Drake got the painkillers and forced one down me. We pushed through the double doors to the outside. It was cold, with a penetrating wind that knew all the defects in my poncho. I hugged it to me, knowing the cold was as much inside as out.

Drake stuffed me into his car, which was parked in the no parking zone right by the door. The seat was sprung, the formerly elegant leather cracked and peeling. It was comfortable, though. I yawned hugely. I would have gone to sleep right where I sat, except for the dull thumping in the back of my head, where the blood pounded through the small mountain my scalp had erected as a monument to pain.

"Well, you'll be fine in a couple of days." Drake pulled out of the parking lot. I closed my eyes.

"Wouldn't want the suspect to be too sick to arrest," I murmured. At the moment, all I wanted was to crawl onto any warm, horizontal surface, and sleep until my head didn't hurt anymore. I didn't want to think about assailants, and murders, and detectives tearing up my bus for the second time in a week. I really didn't want to watch thirty preschoolers cavort around in costume the next day. I just wanted oblivion.

The car didn't ride smoothly, like a well-sprung American car, but I must have fallen asleep anyway. I jolted awake when Drake pulled up in Claudia's drive. He escorted me into the kitchen. Claudia was still there, her arms on either side of a pile of papers on the kitchen table.

Blinking, she looked up when we came in. There were no other policemen in evidence.

"It wouldn't be a good idea to roam around right now," Drake said. He was speaking to both of us.

"I, at any rate, am going nowhere until my ankle heals," Claudia said tartly. "And Liz should go to bed and stay there, too."

"A lot of help I'd be to you under those circumstances." I wanted to argue more, but I could barely force the words out. My eyes started to close without consulting the rest of me.

"Is she all right?" Claudia's voice was alarmed.

"Just a little aftershock," Drake said. His arm came around me again. I was starting to depend on that. His voice sounded very far away. "Where is she going to sleep?"

I pried my eyelids open, but they wouldn't stay. I found myself in the little bedroom off the kitchen. I was in bed. Someone tucked me in. That brief warmth on my lips must have been a kiss. Before I could respond to it, I was asleep.

22

I dreamed that I was lying in my narrow bunk. The attendants were looking in at me through the peephole in the door, and I knew, the way you do in dreams, that I had to pretend that I was still asleep. My body was heavy, and I lay as straight as if in a coffin. I could hear them talking; I kept my eyes closed. Then I realized I couldn't open my eyes, couldn't move hand or foot. They were going to roll me off the bed like a log, take me to the crematorium, even though I wasn't dead, because I couldn't move to save myself.

This is a dream. Open your eyes. It was an incredibly welcome thought, but it took a few moments before I could convince my eyelids they weren't paralyzed. The voices I heard resolved themselves into Bridget and Claudia.

"She doesn't look good." That was Bridget. "Should she be so pale?"

"She's fine. Maybe had a little concussion." Claudia's voice was bracing. "Those nincompoops at the hospital don't know anything. Probably should have kept her there overnight."

"I'm fine." The white plaster ceiling was high above my bed, instead of the low wood paneling in my bus, instead of the cold gray concrete of my dream. There were spider webs in the corners, and an ornate glass light fixture in the center, its base painted over. I was lying between sheets, not in my sleeping bag. They smelled faintly of lavender.

Bridget sat on the edge of the bed. "Are you okay? You look uncomfortable."

"My head hurts." It did. Also my throat, which felt like I'd been eating gravel. Also my teeth, which I'd evidently been grinding in the night. "Not much. I'll be fine."

Claudia limped over and put a glass of orange juice on the little table next to the bed. "You'll live. Do you want to go back to sleep?"

"No!" I shivered, and sat up, trying to move my head as little as possible. Bridget hopped up, and by the time I was halfway through the orange juice, she'd brought me some aspirin. Claudia took her place on the bed, patting my hand a little awkwardly. I blinked fast.

"Look," I said, not meaning to sound so gruff, "I'm not an invalid."

"Of course not." Bridget looked at her watch. "I just stopped in for a minute. Moira has a checkup before the party, so I have to get going. Can I get anything for you two non-invalids?"

"No." I swung my legs over the side of the bed. "After a shower, I'll be perfectly fine. No need to worry, Biddy."

"And my ankle feels much better." Claudia's glare dared us to contradict her. "I'll be in the garden today." She grinned at me. "Can't put off the hybridizing much longer, or it will be too late. Will you have time to work with me on it tomorrow?"

"Sure." I held my head in my hands for a few minutes to clear it, and when I looked up Bridget had brought me some clean clothes from my bus. That meant I didn't have to see the mess the cops had made of it until I was better fortified to face it. I would have to do laundry soon, too. There was the party at the preschool later, and the receding goal of finishing my article for *Smithsonian*. The deadline was still a month away, but I needed time to assemble all the information for the fact-checkers, and time to let the writing sit for a while. Then all the clinkers would sink to the bottom, where I could strain them out with little effort.

Hot water is a wonderful thing. I don't see how humanity survived all those eons without showers.

When I got out to the kitchen, Bridget was gone. Claudia had a bowl of corn flakes in front of her, eating absent-mindedly while reading a glossy journal from the American Society of Historians and Historiographers. She waited until I'd helped myself to corn flakes and brewed a cup of tea before she shut the journal.

"Detective Morales took away the bag you found in your cooler," she mentioned.

"The seeds or whatever?" I poured milk on the cereal and choked down a bite. I wasn't hungry, but experience had taught me that a person needs fuel to be ready for life.

"They were probably some kind of poisonous seed." Claudia pushed the journal away and set her cereal bowl on top of it, so she could lean both elbows on the table. "Might even be yew seeds. Yew is pretty common around here."

"Yew seeds." I crunched another bite and thought about

it. "How would you get them—collect the berries or something? Why not just use those?"

"The seeds are really powerful." Claudia regarded me intently. "When I was in high school, a girl who was trying to give herself an abortion drank tea made from yew seeds and died. The old wives used to use it for that, you see, but they must have made it pretty weak."

I put my spoon down. "Claudia, are you saying someone harvested their ornamental shrubs and planted them on me?"

"Looks that way."

I thought about that bag. It had been an ordinary plastic plastic bag, such as people can buy anywhere. Not me, though; they cost way too much. I use the same plastic bags over and over, to save having to buy them.

"So I guess that must be what killed Alonso," I muttered, watching the corn flakes grow soggy in their milk bath. One crispy little devil had the nerve to float. I picked up my spoon again and pushed it under. "I'm being set up for that."

"And don't forget your Pigpen," Claudia said briskly. Her eyes were bright with interest. "Wasn't he supposed to have been poisoned first? I'm not real clear on the symptoms of yew seeds, but I believe they start pretty quickly after being eaten."

I pushed the bowl of drowning corn flakes away. "Can I use your car, Claudia? I'm going to the preschool for the party."

"It's only nine," she pointed out, heaving herself to her feet. "I thought it didn't start till ten. And you're not driving yourself anywhere with a broken head. I'll drive you. Meanwhile, why don't you rest?"

It occurred to me that Claudia hadn't been out of the house in days. She probably had cabin fever. So I didn't protest her plan.

The tea was hot and steaming and made me feel better. I carried a cup of it out to the bus.

The chaos wasn't so great this time around. The uniforms had tossed it with more sensitivity or something. My underwear still occupied the little drawer under the backseat, instead of being festooned all over the place. It only took fifteen minutes to get everything in place, find my notes on the *Smithsonian* article, and cram the dirty laundry into an empty pillowcase. It would be a boring morning for Claudia, but speaking for myself, I could use more boredom in my life.

23

I called Vivien when I came back in to tell her we were on our way to pick her up for the party. There was no answer. I didn't worry about it too much—she works in her yard and doesn't even try to get the phone if she's very far away.

There was no answer again when I called just before we left.

"I don't like it," I said, putting the receiver down.

Claudia looked up from a plate of toast, which she ate, in the way solitary people have, while reading her historical journal. "Maybe she went to the Senior Center instead—got confused or something."

It was a good thought. I called the desk at the Senior Center, but the woman on duty didn't know Vivien by sight and had no idea if she was there.

"Listen." I grabbed my bag. "You don't need to drive me around. I feel perfectly fine now."

"I'd enjoy it." Claudia managed to look hurt. "What's the matter—would my driving make you nervous?"

"Not at all," I fibbed politely. "I wanted to swing by Vivien's place, that's all. Maybe her phone's out of order."

"Fine with me." Claudia crammed the last bite of toast into her mouth. "You don't mind if I tag along?"

I didn't mind, which surprised me. A week ago I would have felt uncomfortable with so much companionship. Making conversation is a tremendous strain when you've grown accustomed to solitude. Claudia's company was acceptable partly because she didn't put out any kind of demand. She said what she had to say and didn't care if you answered her or not. But underlying my acceptance of this was an uneasy feeling of violent change taking place deep inside, where its mutation would be barely perceptible until it burst forth in some unexpected way.

Claudia drove. Her approach to this was intuitive, making every journey breathtaking, like a reality-based roller coaster. We pulled up outside of Vivien's house with a flourish and, on my part, a sigh of relief.

The shades were still pulled down. When I knocked, no one answered. Because I was uneasy, I turned the door handle. It was locked.

Everyone with an elderly parent or friend would get the same picture—a slip, a fall, a helpless old person on the floor with a broken hip or head. Remembering what Ted Ramsey had said, I called her name a couple of times, listening carefully, but heard nothing.

"She must have left for the party already." I slid into the front seat next to Claudia.

"If she's not there, send your tame policeman to break into the house," she advised, starting the car with a lurch. We careened through the streets north of University, fortunately encountering little traffic. I could have kissed the curb in front of the church where the preschool was located when we got there safely.

Vivien wasn't mingling with the group of elderly ladies and men who ladled punch and dispensed orange-frosted cupcakes. Bridget, who was flying around sticking on Band Aids, hosing off frosting, and mediating arguments, hadn't

114

seen her. I told Bridget I'd be back in a few minutes and went to the phone in the tiny office.

Drake wasn't too interested in my elderly lady friend. "Does it have some bearing on the case?"

"How could it?" I gripped the receiver. "Look, I can just break into her house myself."

"Don't do that!" He sounded alarmed. "At least, don't tell me about it." A heavy sigh came over the line. "Okay, I'll send someone to check it out. But this sort of thing isn't really the province of the police, you know."

"It's just something humans do for each other," I said, holding the door shut to drown out some of the incredible noises from the party. "Thanks a bunch. I'm at the pre-school, in case she's broken her hip or something and needs help checking into the hospital."

Drake didn't sound happy when he said good-bye. I, however, felt much better when I rejoined the party. Claudia had taken one look at the mayhem and retreated to the car with her papers, and Vivien would be taken care of. I settled into a circle with Mick on my lap and joined an enthusiastic rendition of "Six Little Witches."

We went on to "Five Little Pumpkins," and were just starting "Chicken Lips and Lizard Hips and Alligator Thighs" when Drake pushed through the door. Claudia was behind him, her face for once shaken out of its impassivity.

I had risen to my feet before anyone spoke, summoned by the intensely bad vibes that came into the room with Drake. Mick, dumped on the floor, looked indignant, but Bridget beckoned him, watching Drake with a worried frown. Claudia sank into a tiny chair by the door. "I'll take over for you," she whispered, fanning herself. "Go with Drake."

I shut the door on the rousing chorus and followed Drake out to his car.

"It's Vivien, isn't it?" I didn't wait for him to stick me into his battered Saab. "Is she—she isn't dead?"

"Not yet." He faced me on the sidewalk. "It's bad, Liz. I'm taking you to the station."

"I want to see Vivien." I dug my heels in when he took my arm. "Where is she? What happened?"

His breath hissed out in an impatient sigh. "I'll tell you in the car. Come on."

The passenger seat was covered with papers and legal pads and file folders. He heaved them into the backseat and pushed me in. I stared out the dusty windshield while he settled himself behind the wheel. He didn't start the engine.

"Your friend Vivien was unconscious. The officer I sent to check her house managed to unlock the door with a passkey and found her in the living room."

"Did she fall? Was it—"

"It wasn't a fall, we're pretty sure, or at least if she fell, it was because she was already very ill." He darted a glance at me. "There were—unmistakable signs."

"Signs of what?" I pictured Vivien's head beaten in as Pigpen's had been, her skin blue and cold like Alonso's. Inside me was a vast sinking, like being in an elevator at the top of a very tall building, going down very fast.

"Signs of poisoning." He glanced at me again. "Same as Alonso."

Horrified, I met his eyes. "Alonso—but how can that be? She didn't have anything to do with him—with any of that—are you sure? It wasn't just a stroke or a seizure?"

He shrugged and started his car. "We're checking. The medical examiner is, anyway. But I'm pretty sure, yes. That's why I'm taking you to the office."

My elevator hit bottom with a terrible thud. "You think it's me," I said dully. "That I'm the common thread. That I'm poisoning people all over town—street people, people I like."

He pulled up in front of City Hall. "I haven't told you what I think. That would be against the regulations." He came around and opened my door, hauling me out of the car when I didn't move fast enough to suit him. "But I will tell you this. You may not be the common denominator. But you know where it is."

I began to protest, but he kept hustling me up the stairs.

"You may not know what you know," he grumbled in my ear, whisking me down the hall. "But there has to be something we've overlooked, something that ties that old lady to the other deaths. Otherwise—"

He didn't finish the sentence. I dropped into the chair beside his desk and finished it for him. "Otherwise, it comes down to me."

" 'Fraid so." He picked up his phone and growled into it, and moments later Bruno Morales popped in through the door. "Now," said Paul Drake, tipping back his chair and flashing his granny glasses at me. "Let's get down to it."

24

"WE wanted to question your ex-husband, but he doesn't seem to be at his address in Fort Collins."

I was already wrung out by the time Drake made this scary announcement. I had gone through my movements for the last twenty-four hours, a task made easier because Drake witnessed some of that time. We had discussed the mysterious bag that had been found in my bus, and I had said right up front what Claudia suspected, that they were yew seeds. This raised a few eyebrows, and necessitated more phone calls to the labs, endless time on hold, lots of half-voiced cursing and finger-tapping at the bureaucratic delays. During this time, I went off with a couple of female officers for a very complete search of my person and effects.

After it was over, I wanted some intensive privacy, preferably accompanied by soap and hot water. What I got was another one of those Syrofoam cups of Red Zinger and a little downtime in the ladies' room, reflecting while I occupied a stall that being a lady would be pretty easy if everyone else in the world was also required to consult Miss Manners. I had created a pleasing fantasy where attorneys were replaced by etiquette mavens, when my companion, one of the female officers, indicated that I should wrap things up. She was apologetic, and also a little embarrassed by the whole process.

"They've got new technology that's going to make that kind of stuff obsolete," she assured me earnestly as I washed my hands and splashed warm water on my face.

"The sooner the better." I blotted my face with paper towels. The coarse brown paper felt abrasive against my hot forehead. "Do you do this often?"

She looked away from the mirror, where we'd been conducting our conversation. "There's not much call for that around here," she muttered. "Usually anyone who requires a thorough search would be taken to the county for booking."

There was still something to be thankful for—I wasn't being booked. I was simply an involuntary consultant, for the time being. More than anything, I wanted to unearth some fact, some inference, that would avert the forfeit hanging over my head. It's so much easier to convict someone the second time.

Drake told me about Tony when I got back to his office. I had expected something of the sort—had been waiting for the past few days for them to let me know that Tony was in the neighborhood. My life had gotten to such a point that I would almost have welcomed the news as giving the police a fresh new suspect to run around after.

"He's coming after me. He found out the Palo Alto police were making inquiries about me, and now he's on his way." I looked at my hands to avoid looking at Bruno Morales, and especially at Drake. This time, I thought, when Tony showed up, I would stop running away. I wouldn't fight it anymore. I would just let him kill me.

"We'll be doing frequent patrols past Mrs. Kaplan's

house." I looked up in time to catch Drake's thin smile. "She'll enjoy that, no doubt."

Thinking of Claudia, I remembered why I was there. I couldn't believe I'd forgotten Vivien, although a strip search will take your mind off almost anything. "How is Vivien? Can I go see her? Would you take me to see her?"

They glanced at each other, avoiding my eyes. "She's dead, isn't she?" I pressed the heels of my hands hard against my eyes. Images of Vivien swam against my closed eyelids—making tea in her kitchen, pressing me to have a slice of cake, chiding me gently because I didn't find a nice man and settle down. She had done so much for me, and I hadn't been there to help her when she needed help.

The silence in the room told me all I needed to know. "If I had gone by sooner—if she'd had help right away— would she have lived?"

Drake cleared his throat. "Probably not. Once she'd ingested the poison, it would damage her system. She was old. Her chances weren't good at all."

I wouldn't cry there in front of them. Instead, rage filled me. "Why don't you do something, then?" Drake's blank face and Bruno Morales's sympathetic one were the targets of my anger. "Why don't you get out there and find whoever's doing this? It isn't fair that bums and old ladies are taken out, and you can't think of anything better to do than turn your damned bureaucracy loose on me. Why? Why would anyone kill a sweet, quiet lady like Vivien? Why don't you find out?"

They were silent for a moment. "We're trying to," Drake said, pushing his glasses up on his nose. I had a momentary glimpse of those steel-gray eyes. They looked weary and vulnerable. "That's what we need from you. The reason."

"I don't know it!" In despair, I sat down and hid my face in my arm. "I don't know anything about it."

"You knew her," Morales pointed out in his soft voice. "You knew the other victims, too, or at least knew of them. Something links it all."

I was barely listening. Once I got my face under control,

119

I had a sip of the cold Red Zinger. "My class is going to need new members," I muttered, thinking of Vivien's autobiography ending so violently. "First Eunice, and now Vivien."

"Someone else in your class died recently?" Drake leaned forward, his voice sharpening.

"Eunice? She was pretty feeble, too." I glanced from him to Morales. "She was in a wheelchair, had a stroke or something. I don't really know the details. She was doing a great job writing poetry, though."

Once again the men exchanged glances. It made me nervous. "You don't think I'm going around knocking off the members of my workshop, do you?" I gripped the arms of my chair. "For one thing, I need the income. If I killed everyone, I wouldn't get paid for the workshop."

"It's a link." Bruno scribbled down Eunice's full name and went off to get some information.

"She died a natural death," I said, scowling at Drake. "I didn't even hear about it until after the memorial service."

"Vivien's death might have been put down to stroke or heart attack if it hadn't happened around this other stuff," he said.

"You mean, if I hadn't been involved." He didn't contradict it. "How much longer before you arrest me?"

He scowled, turning away. "We don't answer questions like that."

Squabbling sounds came from the hall, and Claudia surged into Drake's tiny office, closely followed by the clerk. "She insisted on seeing you, Detective Drake," the clerk squeaked. "I couldn't stop her."

"Well, Liz." Claudia treated the clerk and Drake with magnificent disregard. "Do you need a lawyer, or are they about ready to let you go home?"

"You're out of line here, Mrs. Kaplan." Drake spoke mildly, but the pencil he was holding snapped in two. "We're not hot-boxing Liz. She wants to clear all this up as much as we do."

"Well, if you have any more questions, you can ask them

at my house. Liz is close to exhausted, as you could see if your glasses were any good." The look she threw him was not friendly. "She's not going to run away."

"Vivien's dead, Claudia." I stared at my hands again, noticing a little line of dirt under my left index fingernail. "They want to find out if I did it."

"And how would you do it, when you were assaulted yourself yesterday?" Claudia snorted. "Are you charging Liz? If not, she's coming with me."

There was a long silence while Drake and Claudia stared at each other. "She can go," he said finally. "But," he added, turning to me, "you're not to be gallivanting around. Stay at Mrs. Kaplan's, since she's making herself responsible for you. Don't go anywhere. If anything out of the ordinary happens, call immediately." He picked up the broken pencil, looked at it as if wondering what had happened, and scrawled a phone number on a page torn from his "Far Side" desk calendar. "Don't eat anything that arrives in the mail or as a delivery. Don't do anything stupid."

Claudia waved all this away. "We'll be in touch," she said carelessly, taking my arm. I was glad of her presence, glad she was battling on my behalf. A grayish fatigue had settled down on me, making it hard to stand and walk.

Drake came behind us down the hall. "I should lock you up for your own safety," he muttered into my ear.

It was tempting for a moment to relinquish to him, to the system, to sit in a cell and let the process swirl around me. Then I saw myself in that little cell, and realized that I couldn't give up, not yet, not ever. "I don't want to be locked up," I said, staring him in the glasses. "I would die."

He blinked, and again I saw that uncertainty. "Oh, pour on the melodrama," he scoffed, but he squeezed my hand briefly before holding open the door. "Remember what I said, or you just might be the next to go. And that would make me seriously annoyed."

25

CLAUDIA detoured downtown and swooped into a fortuitous parking place in front of the Golden Crescent. "I need doughnuts," she muttered, hauling her handbag off the seat between us.

"I'll get them." Despite Claudia's increased mobility, it was my job to gofer.

"I can manage to hobble ten feet to the bakery." Claudia sounded huffy. She pushed the button on her collapsible cane and planted it firmly on the pavement.

"You shouldn't be walking around so much. I thought the doctor said to stay off that foot."

"I'm using the cane." Claudia flourished it triumphantly. "Actually, I've grown to like the cane. Very convenient for enforcing my point of view."

"Okay, okay." I didn't want to get out of the car, really. What I wanted was to crawl into my bus and hibernate for a while, away from all contact with civilization. If I couldn't have that, the front seat of a banged-up Honda would have to suffice.

Claudia stuck her head back into the car. "Now don't go anywhere, Liz. If you're gone when I come back I'll assume you've been abducted by the murderer, and call Detective Drake."

"I'm not stupid," I grumbled, making myself comfortable. "I won't blow it. And—um, I like the buttermilk bars."

I watched Claudia through the bakery window while she pointed to things, and tried not to think about Vivien. Next door to the bakery, the card shop had witches and goblins and pumpkins plastered all over its windows. Walgreen's on the corner had draped its display area with cheap costumes and pyramids made from bags of candy. Halloween makes me nervous—it's a difficult holiday for someone who doesn't live in a house. The only good thing about it, from my point of view, is that after it's over, the candy goes on sale. The little Milky Ways are my weakness. Vivien liked the Three Musketeers—"They don't bother my dentures," she'd told me once.

Try as I might to think of something else, Vivien's gentle face and voice filled my head. I put a hand over my eyes and wished I'd stayed at the police station. Though there wasn't much I could contribute to the investigation, something might have come up that would help. Instead I'd allowed Claudia to drag me off and stuff me with undeserved treats. My eyes felt gritty; I thought of that bottle of painkillers the hospital had given me. Two of those and I could check out of my troubles until tomorrow. There were only ten in all—not enough for permanent sleep.

Claudia was still haranguing the woman behind the counter in the Golden Crescent. The sidewalks were full of people, a motley group of business suits both male and female, moms pushing strollers, older kids rollerblading and carrying skateboards, and a generous sprinkling of what the press likes to call the disadvantaged, some wearing clothes so ancient and dirty I could smell them from inside the car, pushing shopping carts filled with their possessions, checking out the trash receptacles along the sidewalk. I saw Old Mackie shambling along, his bottle snuggled into a paper bag in the front of his shopping cart. Weird Sam was beside him. It struck me that I was out of the loop in my community—not that I'd ever been deeply into it, but if these murders hadn't involved me, I'd know all the gossip about Alonso and Pigpen, what was being said on the street, how much fear of the killer was affecting my vagrant kin. I would even be a little afraid myself, if it wasn't for being so closely involved that I was a lot afraid.

Delores Mitchell came out of Walgreen's, her nostrils looking distressed as Old Mackie wheeled past her. I sank deeper in my seat, hoping to evade her notice. It didn't work. She stood right in front of Claudia's car, waiting for the light to change so she could cross the street to the Federated Savings office. Glancing around impatiently while she waited, she saw me.

She smiled and came to tap gaily at the window until I rolled it down. "Hi, Liz. You're in the passenger seat! Are you being chauffeured around? I never get to the bottom of you!"

"I wouldn't even bother." I tried not to sound as hostile as I felt. Delores was chic as ever in a bright fuchsia jacket with black trim and a short black skirt that showed off her well-exercised legs. Her Walgreen's bag banged against the side of the car and she tucked it under her arm. Through the thin plastic of the bag I could see what it contained. "Delores—Reese's peanut butter cups? Don't they promote cellulite?"

She laughed a little self-consciously. "For the trick-or-treaters." Her laugh died, and she looked earnestly at me. "I heard about Vivien. You must be feeling so bad, Liz. I know how fond of her you were."

"She was a great person." I didn't want to discuss Vivien with Delores, whose responses always seemed tried on, as if she was shopping for the right thing to say.

"Well, no one lives forever." Delores sighed heavily. "She was old. It was only a question of time." Once more she peered earnestly at me. "Will your class keep on? I heard they weren't going to give space to any group with less than ten students. How many do you have now? Maybe I could send you someone. I have a few elderly clients at the bank who might enjoy writing."

"Thanks, Delores." I reminded myself that grinding my teeth was bad for them. "I'll manage." Spotting Claudia coming through the door of the Golden Crescent, I sighed with relief. "Here comes my ride. I won't keep you any more."

Delores looked at the big box Claudia carried. "She must be having a party. So, are you staying with her?" Her eyes rounded, and she blushed. "I didn't mean—I meant, is she hiring you—well, I worry about you, Liz. It's just—nice that you've found a place. Off the street." She blinked soulfully at me. "Vivien would have been pleased." Claudia, coming out of the bakery, got the tail end of a misty smile as Delores passed, her heels clicking on the sidewalk.

"Who was that?" Claudia got into the car, handing me the box.

"Delores Mitchell. She's some kind of veep at Federated Savings. I know her from the Senior Center; she gives financial planning seminars there."

"Mitchell." Claudia stared after Delores's perky, retreating figure. "Her dad must have been old Stewart Mitchell. We got our first home loan from Federated. He was quite a guy—real macho type. Died from lung cancer a couple of years ago." She shook her head and pulled away from the curb. "I remember sitting in his office, pregnant with Carlie, and Stewart was blowing smoke rings with the smelliest cigar I ever choked on. He wasn't thrilled when I asked him to put it out." Ahead of us, Delores crossed the street and vanished into the Federated office. "He should have left it out."

Inelegantly, my stomach growled. I fingered the string around the doughnut box. It was almost noon. My body was hungry, but the notion of eating repelled me. I was tired, but unable to rest. So deeply frightened I was numb.

At least that's what I thought. But a ride with Claudia driving had a way of separating the truly suicidal from those merely flirting with the idea. By the time Claudia parked in her driveway, I was grateful still to be alive. She limped up the steps, grumbling about the moron in the BMW who'd contested the last stop sign with her. She, of course, had won. In any encounter like that, the person who wants to keep his car in one piece is at a disadvantage.

Claudia put the kettle on, and I moved around, spooning coffee into a filter, finding myself a tea bag, trying to make the world normal. When I turned back to the table, cups in hand, she had opened the doughnuts and positioned a fresh pad of paper and a couple of newly sharpened pencils in front of her on the table.

"Thanks," she said, accepting her coffee and plopping an enormous cinnamon roll on a napkin. "Help yourself." She took a bite of roll and picked up a pencil. "I figure we have an hour at most. So let's get started."

I blew on my tea to cool it. "Started with what? I thought I was supposed to take a nap."

She shot me an impatient look. "Don't be dense, Liz. Your policeman will be by soon enough to check up and make sure you're playing by the rules. In the meantime, we can make some progress without getting tangled up in their ridiculous bureaucracy." She wrote the date of Pigpen Murphy's last encounter with the world at the top of her paper in big letters. "Now. Tell me everything. The police believe there's a clue somewhere in your memory. We're going to find it."

26

"I'VE read a lot of mysteries." Claudia took the cap off her pen. I reached for my knapsack and pulled out my own little notebook. If there was note-taking going on, I wanted to be part of it.

"Mysteries aren't like life, Claudia." I found my razor-point and faced her across the table. "In mysteries you have red herrings and plots. Here it's all a mishmash. If the same person is doing this, which is by no means certain, what could possibly be the link between people like Pigpen and Vivien?"

"That's what we're going to find out." Claudia began making lines on her tablet. "Pigpen's was the first death. Let's go back to that. What exactly did he say to you that night? Maybe there's a clue in there."

Her obvious relish for the exercise was the only thing that made me cooperate. I was sick of it all. Murder or death—it all began to seem irrelevant. We're all dying; some of us just go faster than others. Vivien shouldn't have died, but she was old and had often said she was ready to go when her time came. Alonso was too young to die, but on the other hand he wasn't making much of his life. Pigpen was simply a blot on the landscape. Was that how the murderer had felt?

Claudia echoed my thoughts. "A person might think they were just putting people like Pigpen Murphy and Alonso out of their misery," she remarked, scribbling busily. "Kind of tidying up Nature's mistakes."

"Unless they cooperated in the process, it's still murder," I pointed out. "I don't want anyone standing in judgment of my life and deciding whether or not I deserve it."

"Naturally," Claudia said, faintly scandalized. "I wasn't suggesting that such a course of action would be allowable. I was just trying to put myself in the murderer's shoes."

The murderer's shoes. Tony's boots made an appearance in my mental movie. He had gotten a construction job, even though he was too good for that kind of manual labor, and steel-toed boots were required. The job had lasted a couple of weeks, until he'd picked a fight with the supervisor. The boots lasted much longer. He would sit in the kitchen to clean them, rubbing the saddle soap into their creases. He even named them. "The shit-kickers," he called them, lacing them up before he went drinking with his buddies. I knew he found them useful in brawls—those steel toes could really inflict pain. One morning after he'd come back from drinking and shown me how much pain, I had crawled off the living room sofa, and, moving carefully so as not to aggravate my newly bruised ribs, mixed up a gallon of Fix-All and poured it into his boots. That was the first time I left him.

Now I had to shut my eyes to stop the memory. Did he know where I was? Was it his hand I detected in these deaths—a gradual progression that would lead him to me? "I'm putting you in danger," I said, rubbing my eyes. "First Vivien, then you, then me. I should leave."

"You weren't living with Vivien," Claudia pointed out. "No offense, Liz, but I believe you're taking too egocentric a view of the events here. Perhaps they have nothing to do with you."

"They have me nearly arrested." I put down my pen and felt gently around the back of my head. There was still a big knot there, the source of the headache that throbbed like a monotonous conga drum inside my skull. "Someone wants me out of the way—either in prison or dead. We both know that."

Claudia leaned back with every appearance of enjoyment. "Now that's where I think you're wrong. I don't think this murderer wants you dead at all. This is a pretty efficient killer, by all the evidence. If you were supposed to die, I think it would already have been arranged." She took a big bite of doughnut. "My take on it is that you're more valuable as a scapegoat than a victim. As long as you can't put your finger on the common thread, you're not a threat to the murderer. But if he can arrange to pin it on you—"

"An interesting theory." Paul Drake spoke from the kitchen door. We both turned and gaped at him. I hadn't heard a sound—he must have walked on the grass of the driveway to avoid the crunching gravel.

"You're certainly sneaky, Detective Drake." Claudia regarded him with disapproval. "And you're early."

He blinked. Some of the sternness went out of his face. "You were expecting me?"

"I figured you'd be around to pick Liz's brain, since you didn't get a chance at the station." Claudia gestured magnificently toward the box of doughnuts. "Why else would I have gotten a dozen of these dangerous objects?"

Drake looked hungrily at the box. "You should have your doors locked," he said, coming into the kitchen and demonstrating his point by locking the door behind him. He marched into the hall, and we could hear him checking the front door. "Even if there wasn't someone out there knocking off Liz's friends." His voice floated down the hall to us, and then he came back in. "You should still keep your door locked." He sat down at the table and pulled the box toward him. "Is there any coffee?"

I exchanged a look with Claudia and got a cup for Drake out of the dish drainer, pushing the carafe of coffee toward him. He sniffed it dubiously. "Who made this?"

"I did." I poured him a cup. "Do you dare to drink it?"

"As long as it isn't Mrs. Kaplan's instant," he answered cheerfully. Claudia tried not to smile.

"Have I ever told you, Detective, how much I deplore your manners?"

"Actually, I think you have." He deliberated over the box, finally choosing a cinnamon twist. When he bit into it, his eyes closed. Even his granny glasses looked blissful. "Heavenly," he breathed. "Is there any milk?"

This time I just pointed to the refrigerator. He waited on himself, and when he came back to the table he took a minute to look at Claudia's notes. "Very neat," he said approvingly. "Nice chart. Just like a mystery."

Suspecting sarcasm, Claudia scowled at him. "Organization is the key to any scholarly undertaking," she sniffed. "Perhaps you'd already have this killer behind bars if you tried it, Detective Drake."

"I have my own methods," he said, putting the doughnut down. "One of them is to interview those who might have important information. If you don't want to go back to the station, Ms. Sullivan, you're going to have to answer my questions fully and completely, with no interference." He darted a look at Claudia, who raised her eyebrows innocently. "I prefer that spectators leave the room."

"It's my kitchen." Claudia settled herself deeper into her chair and crossed her arms over her massive bosom. "And I intend to keep you from badgering my friend."

Drake sighed impatiently. "This is not a game, Mrs. Kaplan. Your friend is in big trouble. I'm trying to help, which means I'm looking to uncover the truth. I do Liz the courtesy of believing that the truth will in her case make her free, and not a future resident of one of our over-crowded correctional institutes. So butt out or shut up; I don't much care which."

To my surprise, Claudia did not rip Drake's head off—verbally, of course; she would never attempt physical violence. She simply picked up her pen, turned to a fresh page in her notebook, and waited silently.

Drake took me through everything Pigpen had said, everything I had said. At least, what I thought I'd said. As in any event under constant scrutiny, the reality had been replaced by the official version. I couldn't really tell any more if those were his exact words, my exact words. What I remembered with clarity about that evening was the quality of the light, pouring through the trees to gild the steep sides of the creek, highlighting the fall brilliance of the poison oak that clothed it. I remembered the smell of the pine trees and the way my pear had tasted. And that Mrs. Gaskell wrote of the graveyard that reared its stones under Charlotte Brontë's bedroom window. And how Pigpen's unwashed body smell fought with the mothball scent of his Goodwill ensemble.

Drake wanted all that, too. He was the best listener I'd ever had. Certainly better than the lawyer appointed by the court to defend me from attempted murder charges against my ex-husband. Drake listened as if every action recounted, every thought rethought, would go directly into his bank account and be turned into gold.

It was the same with my encounter with Alonso. What he'd said to me, and I to him, was incidental. How he looked, the way he clutched the paper bag to his chest as if I'd challenge him for the cereal samples he'd been stealing, the macabre way his new outfit mirrored Pigpen's, even down to the mothball smell, were all displayed for Drake's benefit and Claudia's notes.

"You mentioned the mothballs before." Drake had a notepad, too, a very small one on which he made undecipherable marks with a mechanical pencil. He thumbed back through the little pages, dislodging a few, until he found one he wanted. "We contacted Goodwill," he said, blinking at me from behind his glasses. "They don't use mothballs."

"I smelled them," I insisted stubbornly. "And they were both wearing relatively clean pants and newish-looking shoes. Pigpen had enormous feet."

Drake didn't really seem to need his notes. "You said Pigpen wore a flight jacket over the kind of vest that comes in a three-piece suit."

"No." I shook my head. "He wore a flight jacket. It was zipped. I didn't see what was underneath, and I didn't want to find out."

Drake made another notation and seemed to hesitate for a moment. "Well, here's an interesting fact for you. The vest Pigpen wore matched the suit jacket Alonso had on when he died. Both of them had all labels removed. And you were right. Both smelled a little of mothballs."

I thought that over, but Claudia got there first. "So the same source provided their new clothes. So they must have been working together."

"What kind of work was that?" It didn't make sense. "No one would bother to dress up to steal those cereal samples. Alonso was certainly doing it on a grand scale, but that kind of stuff is fair game, especially if it's just crammed into the newspaper bin underneath apartment mailboxes."

"What would you think Pigpen and Alonso would do if they were given a temporary job, some money?"

I hesitated. "If I were looking to bootstrap some homeless people, I wouldn't have picked either of those two," I finally said. "There are some that are on the street because they don't have any choices, and there are some that have chosen the street."

"And Pigpen was the latter?"

"Well, he wasn't reliable." I didn't like having to dish about the street. There are remarkably decent people who have taken blow after blow from life until all they have left is a car or a shopping cart or just a blanket. They have stopped trying to elude their fate; they accept it at the same time that they turn away from it to drugs or liquor or whatever cheap escape their meager resources offer. Alonso had seemed to me to be coming from that perspective, handicapped by his rather trusting dimness. Pigpen, however, had been a natural-born bum, someone to whom work wasn't worthwhile unless it was money for nothing. "If he'd ever gotten a job, I'd expect him to just take the first paycheck and drink it up and never show up again."

"Sounds like he was blackmailing someone, not working," Claudia observed. "All that about going to the bank—he had something on someone, and whoever it was killed him."

"Like maybe knowledge of someone's criminal record?" I forced the words out through my tight throat. "Maybe he told Alonso and that's why I had to off him, too."

"We thought about that." Drake leaned back in his chair and took another bite of doughnut, chewing thoughtfully, as if our discussion was simply academic. "But there didn't seem to be any reason why you'd kill to conceal your record. And what would be the point of blackmailing you? You don't have any money."

"I have more than most of them," I muttered. For the past few years I had told myself I was one of the people of the street, but now I realized that I didn't want to be classified with losers and drifters. Secretly I had been that far more romantic figure, the fugitive. I was an outcast to my family—jailbirds were definitely not welcome. But I hadn't really sought the company of my homeless companions. I had made my bus a home, even if it was ephemeral compared to the fancy real estate all around Palo Alto. I felt an intense longing for its snug illusion of security, for the sense that I was free, able to head out to fresh horizons at any minute.

But something I'd stifled was rising to the surface, too—a need for people who knew and cared about me, for purpose that transcended the next stopping place. That was what had kept me in Palo Alto—along with the pretense that I was free to move on at any threat, I had enjoyed feeling like part of a community.

"Liz?" Claudia touched my arm, and I realized that my cheeks were wet. "Do you need a break?"

I shook my head and pulled a bandanna out of my pocket. "We aren't finished until we figure out who did it, are we?" I tried a bright smile, and wasn't surprised when it didn't move my companions. "Trapped inside a murder mystery. Is it snowing outside?"

That got a sour smile from Drake. "No, but we're going to force doughnuts down your throat until you talk, shweetheart."

"No need for force." I broke a piece off my buttermilk bar, but couldn't bring it to my mouth. There was a lot I couldn't seem to swallow just then. "Where were we?"

"We were figuring out who Pigpen was blackmailing." Claudia looked back through her notes.

"But what could link Pigpen with Vivien?" I gave up all pretense of eating. "Why would anyone want to kill her?"

Drake cleared his throat. "Some people will do anything for property."

"Vivien's property? Who gets it?" I pushed the plate away and looked at the lukewarm dregs in my teacup.

The quality of Drake's silence alerted me to the danger. I looked at him, and the cold gray eyes were clearly visible behind the lenses. "In her will," he said deliberately, "she leaves her house to you."

27 _____

CLAUDIA choked, and I absently pounded her on the back. I was seeing those black bars again, swimming closer and closer. Vivien had meant to give me a wonderful surprise on the sad occasion of her death, not a motive for murdering her.

"How long have you known this?" I glared at Drake. He was the yo-yo master, and I was the yo-yo; one minute I was up there on his side, the next I was scraping the floor. If the purpose of his technique was to keep me off balance, he was doing a wonderful job.

"It came through just before I came over here." He stared back at me, unwinking. "You deny that you knew?"

"I didn't know." The need for solitude, for time to adjust to all these changes, pressed me. "Poor Vivien. She meant to be so kind."

"Her will says something about the house being yours to sell or live in, though she hopes you will live in it."

"She didn't like my living on the street." I folded my arms and hugged them across my chest, trying not to shiver. "She always wanted me to move into that cottage in the back."

"Why didn't you?" Drake leaned forward, like some kind of twisted therapist.

"Too much money. Not mobile enough," I said dully. "I was afraid of getting an address." The fear seemed stupid now. Either Tony had found me after all and was weaving this delightful plot to trap me, or I had given up the chance to help a very nice person. If I'd been living there, perhaps Vivien wouldn't have been poisoned.

Claudia got up and limped to the stove, returning in a moment with a hot cup of herb tea. "Drink this," she said, glaring at Drake. "You've had a shock."

"It's not as if Liz is suddenly rich," he pointed out. "That old place needs lots of deferred maintenance. The only way you can afford it is to sell it, but you wouldn't get enough out of it to buy a house around here." He leaned forward again. "Of course," he murmured, "you could go somewhere else, where things are cheaper—Oregon, or Colorado—"

"No!" I clutched the warm cup. "How can this happen? How can a loving gesture turn me into an even hotter suspect?"

Claudia looked at me, worried. "It's a shock. But don't collapse, Liz. Use your head. We're going to get at the truth here, if you can help us." She challenged Drake. "Who else knew that Liz was the beneficiary?"

He smiled. "Vivien used a standard will form from the stationer's, so there was no attorney involved. Her son died, you told me, in Korea, so she had no relatives to consider. According to Liz, she wasn't told. So it seems no one knew about it. At least, no one's come forward."

"Delores Mitchell," I said suddenly.

"Who?" Claudia wrote the name down on her pad.

"That woman we saw today—you know, old Stewart Mitchell's daughter. I know Vivien took one of her workshops. Maybe Delores knows something about her will." I remembered something else. "Yes, and I won't get the house anyway," I said triumphantly. "Vivien had taken a reverse mortgage. Those people will get the house."

"They'll put it up for sale," Drake said after a thoughtful silence. "But I think the way that works is they get their advance plus interest out of it, and the rest of the proceeds go to the residual legatee." He wrote Delores's name down too. "I'll check it out."

"So both you and Vivien knew this Mitchell woman."

Claudia gnawed on her pen. "Who else did you both know?"

"Hard to say." I was finding it difficult to focus. The hot tea helped. I closed my eyes. "That developer. Ted Ramsey."

"Ramsey's a friend of yours?" Drake looked up from his notes. "I didn't know that."

"He's not my friend." I struggled to be coherent. "He swims at the same time I do. I met him a couple of times, once when I was taking Vivien to class. He was after her house. Promised to find her a nice studio in one of the ritzy retirement homes around. She was too nice when she turned him down—he kept thinking she just needed a little more persuasion."

"So he wanted her place—why? He doesn't do single-family stuff." Drake made a few notes.

"He had options on a couple of other houses next to hers. The one around the corner belonged to Eunice, the other woman in my writing group that just died. She had a big lot with a small house and her backyard intersected with Vivien's." I remembered yesterday's awkward moment. "One of the other neighbors, Carlotta Houseman, is really gung-ho to move into a retirement place. She was feuding with Vivien because she thought Vivien was going to queer the whole deal." I surprised myself by yawning.

Claudia caught it. "You're tired," she said, putting down her pen. "Why don't you take that nap now?"

"We're not finished." Drake directed an intimidating stare at Claudia. She didn't back down.

"Liz is." She was right. I felt exhausted, in spite of the long sleep the night before. My head throbbed, my eyes felt sandy. I wanted to crawl into my bus and hide in my sleeping bag while crying a couple of gallons of tears for everything that had gone wrong in the universe over the past two billion years.

"I'll come back for dinner," Drake announced, knowing, I guess, that if he waited to be invited he would have a good long wait. "I'll bring a pizza or something. You ladies are not thinking of going out, are you?"

"We women," Claudia told him, heaving herself to her feet to accompany me, "are going to nap and recruit our subconscious brains to do the hard work of figuring out what has been going on here. If the pizza smells good enough, we might let you in."

"Lock the door after me," he ordered, taking another doughnut out of the box and following us out of the kitchen. "Don't let anyone else in. If you remember anything pertinent, don't call up potential blackmailers and tell them about it. Let me know. Let me know if anything worries or bothers you or anyone wants to talk to you. I don't want any accidents happening here, understand?"

"You come in loud and clear, Detective Drake." Claudia stopped in the doorway of the room she'd assigned to me. "We'll see you later."

I barely remember falling onto the bed. Sleep was deep and welcoming, like a thick blanket between me and the rest of the world. I didn't want to dream, but of course I did.

Vivien was standing at the counter in her kitchen, which by the alchemy of dreams I knew was actually my kitchen now. But there she was, fixing me a snack, smiling over her shoulder like she used to do. When she turned around, I saw that instead of the usual plate of sliced cake, she was holding a bowl of cereal, its black blobs of raisins floating in milk. Behind her on the counter was the little sample box. A feeling of horror grew slowly while I stared at the bowl held in her gnarled hands. Reluctantly I shifted my gaze, and there was Alonso, clutching the bag to his chest, glaring at me accusingly. Vivien, too, had lost her smile; she looked as if she disapproved of something. Her hands began to tremble, and I reached for the bowl before the milk could slosh onto the floor, but it receded as I reached, until I wasn't in the kitchen anymore and Vivien, blown before me like a wispy kite, was rapidly borne out of sight. Alonso began to mutate, his face dripping and changing in a grotesque kind of acid flashback. I knew what he would turn into, and told myself to wake up, but not before Pigpen's dead face confronted me, his expression somehow sly, the open eyes filmed over.

I did wake up then. The dream's lingering horror settled over me thickly. I had that groggy, befuddled feeling that comes from sleeping in the daytime. More than anything, I wanted a swim. It was just past one; the pool would still be open for laps.

It didn't take long to strip and put on my suit. Claudia was sleeping; I could hear from the foot of the stairs her deep breathing and occasional delicate snores. All this was a strain on her, and she wasn't in the best of shape to begin with. Obviously she needed her nap more than I'd needed mine.

I pulled sweats over my suit, rolled up a towel, and looked at the back door lock for a minute. The key was in it. Drake would definitely say it was dumb to go for a swim. I wanted to pretend that didn't matter. But to let the antagonism between us color my self-preservation—that would be dumb.

The phone was in the kitchen. I closed the door so I wouldn't wake up Claudia. Drake answered himself, impatiently, as if he'd been interrupted in devising a solution to the national debt.

"Drake. I'm going to Rinconada Pool. I'm riding Claudia's bike—it's less than a mile. I'll be finished in an hour or so, and bike back."

"You're out of your gourd, lady." His breath hissed through the receiver, diving down my ear. "You don't go anywhere or do anything."

"I'm letting you know," I pointed out, realizing how much easier it was to talk to him without his well-honed, inquisitive presence. "I could have just left, and no one the wiser."

"Where's your keeper?" He sounded seriously annoyed. "I thought the formidable Mrs. Kaplan was going to guard you like a Rottweiler."

I couldn't help the smile. At least he wouldn't see it. "She's getting some rest. I'm not going to bother her, and neither are you."

"So it's not clear who takes the Rottweiler role, is it?" The sounds of paper being shuffled, or perhaps shoveled, filled the receiver. Then he spoke again. "I haven't taken a lunch break yet. I'll pick you up in a few minutes. Don't wait outside, and lock the door when you come out. I'll take you to Rinconada and bring you back."

"I'm touched." A flat voice, reciting orders—I had lived too many years with that already. "Such concern for my well-being. Next time, I won't tell you first."

"There might not be a next time." The frankness was brutal. "Your possible futures include a couple of scenarios that would severely limit your movements."

"You mean jail." I leaned against the wall. "So I'm pretty much under house arrest right now, is that it? I'm surprised you don't have someone posted here."

There was a brief silence, time enough to deduce the bull's-eye. "I'm not talking about jail," he said finally, as if exasperated. "I'm talking about death. Wait inside until you see my car. It's a—"

"I remember your car." My mouth wanted to say something else, but my hand hung up before I could betray myself. I scribbled a note for Claudia and left it in the middle of the kitchen table. Then I unlocked the back door and relocked it after me, pocketing the key. Drake might be concerned for my safety, but he also regarded me as chief suspect. There was sure to be a policeman lurking somewhere. I was in no danger, and there was something I had to do.

My bus was out of sight behind the garage. I ran my hand along the side, feeling the ridges on the metal from my inexpert attempt at painting it last summer. The curtains were pulled back, as I'd left them after tidying up after the assault. The cardboard window still showed its hole from the previous night's break-in; I hadn't yet gotten around to fixing it. I unlocked the door and checked that the cooler

139

door was propped open to air and that everything was in its place. The boxes of files stashed on the floor under the pull-up table gave me a pang. It was as if the life I'd shaped for the past few years was over already, with only a big question mark to take its place. I had found my little rut so comforting, so secure. Now I knew that comfort and security had been delusion and illusion. There was no going back. There might be no going on.

Bereft, rootless, I turned away when I heard the car idling in front of the house, locking up the artifact of my past, going to meet the arbiter of my future.

28

I didn't realize Drake was going to swim, too. I had expected him to wait in the car until I was done, since this kind of embarrassing baby-sitting couldn't be much more to his taste than it was to mine. I would have been flattered by the minuteness of his attention if I hadn't figured that nine-tenths of it was because he didn't want his chief suspect whisked out of reach by accidental drowning.

The other tenth of his interest might possibly be personal.

He was waiting for me outside the women's dressing room when I came out. He stood in the bright, cold October breeze, his legs braced slightly apart, arms crossed over his chest. As I had surmised, his build was burly; he wore baggy, Jams-style trunks instead of the sleek, nut-hugging racing suits the real swim jocks wore. What really made him looked naked was that his glasses were gone. He squinted at me, doing as thorough a catalog as I was. At least he would see me through the soft blur of poor vision. I am not one of those petite women who hang out around Nordstrom, bemoaning the dearth of size twos. My body has been lived in long past any damage a security deposit might cover. And it was never fashionable—though I might have given Rubens or Renoir a little heartache. Hourglass figures don't work in the digital age.

Drake seemed accustomed to the unwritten etiquette of the pool involving lane speed and entry. I like to swim slowly but steadily, so I usually choose a lane near the deep end where the older swimmers go. Drake headed for the middle lanes, faster territory. He pulled on goggles, too; I don't bother with them. If you use goggles and swim caps and floats and special shampoo, swimming ceases to be a cheap form of exercise.

I plowed back and forth through the water, unable to capture the usual mindless content with which I swim. There was too much churning around in my head, too many images, too much sorrow and pain. Swimming should be like meditation—just you, your breath, the rhythmic motion of your arms and legs, the punctuation marks of turns. At least that's how it seemed to me when I discovered lap swimming in college. I've done it ever since, wherever I can find a pool.

After five laps of crawl stroke I switched to breast-stroke. With my head out of the water, I could scan the other lanes. Drake had worked his way over to the lane next to mine—I saw his red swim cap. He was doing side-stroke, watching me. It didn't help my concentration any. I switched to sidestroke, too, turning my back to him.

By lap ten I like to do some backstroke. But an elderly man had gotten into the lane with me, and his scissors kick was a real lane hog. I went back to crawl, burying my face in the water, seeking at least the relaxation that comes with exercise, if I couldn't find the serenity.

I finished a very slow fifteen laps and climbed out of the pool. Drake hauled himself out, too. He'd swum the whole time, and didn't seem winded. I had put him down as soft and sweet-tooth impaired. But his stocky build was all well toned. The only softness came from lots of frizzy, graying chest hair.

"You must work out a lot," I said on the way back to the dressing room. "Swimming can be tiring if you're not used to it."

"I swim," he said curtly. I had never noticed him at the pool, but he probably came early before work. We stopped outside the women's locker room. "I'm trusting you, Liz. Don't leave by the other door."

"I won't." I wanted to say more, to express outrage that he doubted me, to demand that things come to a head so I could know where I stood. But that was obvious—I stood, dripping wet, shivering in the cold breeze, watching goose bumps break out on the parts of Drake's arms that weren't hairy. For once I could see into his eyes with no barriers. And for some reason, I didn't want to look. I turned away, into the echoing dampness of the locker room.

The hard blast of the locker room shower didn't feel nearly so good when it wasn't the only shower in my world. I rinsed off perfunctorily, dried quickly, and pulled a comb through my hair. I keep it short by cutting it myself when it begins to get in my way. This time, on my way out of the locker room, I stopped in front of the mirror. Through the steam that obscured it, I saw my image—short, pale, no makeup, hair ragged. For the past few years I had cultivated looking like nobody, not willing to arouse interest in anyone, especially a man. When I caught myself wondering if I'd overdone it, I marched quickly out, back to my baby-sitter.

Drake was talking to Ted Ramsey, who had just arrived at the pool, judging from his dry condition and the athletic bag he carried. He bent his head attentively to catch Drake's voice and nodded slowly. Ted didn't see me, since Drake moved around a little as I approached so that the developer's back was to me. Drake scowled a little right at me, and I slowed. I could hear Ted answering Drake's question.

142

" . . . certainly is a desirable area," Ted was saying. "It's no secret that I'm interested in a project there. I've got options on a couple of other properties nearby, and I think the neighborhood would support sensitively designed higher-density housing there after the ecological benefits are pointed out."

With some effort I figured out he was talking about Vivien's house. I moved a little closer to hear better. Ted must have had good peripheral vision. He saw me and turned, holding out his hand.

"Liz, how nice to see you. I know you're very distressed about poor Vivien. Her passing is so sad." He glanced from me to Drake. "Is there some—irregularity? Is that why you're asking questions, Paul?"

Drake shrugged. "We have to check out unexpected deaths, Ted. Just thought you might know about the plans for that area. Ms. Sullivan here mentioned that you were trying to work a deal with Mrs. Greely, and that one of her neighbors—Mrs. Houseman—was really pressuring her about it."

"A lot of people know that." Ted regarded me for a moment. "Paul, if you're thinking there might have been foul play, I know that Liz wouldn't have had any part in it. She's just been very devoted to those ladies—Vivien and Eunice, and all of them in her class. Why, even Carlotta admits that—" He stopped short, and I filled in the blanks for myself. Even Carlotta, who hated street people, admitted that good old Liz Sullivan wasn't so bad. Big of her. Ted went on smoothly, "Liz may have an unconventional lifestyle, but she's a fine person."

"Thanks." I raised my eyebrows at Drake, wondering if he'd noticed the very subtle way Ted had linked Vivien's death with Eunice's, and me with both of them. A nice guy, but not one to find himself on a possible limb with me and not try to saw it off.

Drake got the message. His glasses were back in place, but I was starting to read the slightest change in that impassive face, and I thought the tightening of the muscles around his mouth indicated an incipient smile. Knowing that much about a man I'd just met bothered me a lot. He held a tremendous power over my freedom. Perhaps, like a kidnap victim or hostage, I would seek to placate my captor by getting a crush on him. Drake probably didn't find such uncomfortable vibes in our relationship of investigator and suspect.

Soon it would all be resolved, one way or another, and I would no longer need to attach great significance to whether a cop was smiling or frowning.

In the meantime, this cop was in charge of the action, however I might resist that thought. I fully expected him to whip out the handcuffs at some point and haul me away. So it was quite a surprise when he nodded affably and said, "Nice running into you, Liz. Tell Bridget hello for me if you see her."

This unexpected development stymied me for a moment. Drake turned back to his conversation with Ted, and I meandered toward the pool gates. It seemed that Drake didn't want me to be known as chief suspect. Perhaps right now he was assuring Ted Ramsey that the police were inclined to believe Vivien's death was from natural causes.

Delores Mitchell came breezing through the gates before I got to them. She carried a chic leather-banded gym bag which contained, no doubt, an assortment of lotions, shampoos, and cosmetics to protect her from the chlorine, as well as a fine swimsuit and all the other accessories possible. The rank envy I felt for her perfect appearance, her possession of everything that made life easy and comfortable, was an unpleasant emotion; to counter it, I was a little nicer to her than I wanted to be.

"Well, long time no see," Delores said, smiling cordially. "How's the water today? Too much chlorine?"

"No." Her scent, something expensive and complex, drifted to me on the breeze. I even envied that. "Even us no-goggles types can be comfortable today." I smiled, too, trying not to be surly.

"You always look so free with your hair loose in the water." She sighed. "My hair can't take it; if I don't wear a cap I can't do anything with it." Her gaze went past me, and her eyes widened. "Why, Officer Drake, you swim, too? A person meets everyone at the pool."

I stepped aside, and Drake joined us. "I'll say. You didn't mention you were going to swim this afternoon, Miss Mitchell, or I would have offered you a ride."

This unblushing lie caused me not a blink. I was getting good at knowing my role. In fact, I seized on the opportunity to play it. "Hi, Paul," I said eagerly.

"Liz." He nodded casually at me, and I allowed myself to be deflated. "Yes," he went on, aiming the chat at Delores, "I just saw Ted Ramsey getting ready to swim. Real nice guy, even if he is in real estate. You probably know him, too, Miss Mitchell?" He looked at her admiringly.

"Call me Delores." She batted her eyelashes at him, unable to resist a tiny, triumphant glance in my direction, "Yes, we've met a few times—business, you know. But how can you swim, Paul? I got the impression you were knee-deep in figuring out whether poor Vivien's death was natural or not."

"I was." Drake grimaced. "Had to get away for a little while, get some perspective. Well, see you ladies later." He headed out the gates.

"How did you meet him?" Delores gazed after Drake, her face speculative.

"He knows Bridget Montrose." I was telling the truth, although not the whole truth. "How did you meet him?"

"Cute guy," she decided. "A little shaggy, though. He dropped by the office and talked to me earlier. About Vivien's reverse mortgage, and her state of mind—you know. You've probably talked to him, too—in his official capacity." Again her look was speculative, though directed at me.

"I've given the police some information," I said vaguely.

"Well, I have to get my swim." She looked past me, and I looked around, too. Ted Ramsey was striding toward the pool from the men's dressing room, his body long and lean in a skimpy racing suit, his towel slung rakishly across his chest. He was heading for the fast lanes, of course. I'd bet anything that Delores found herself there, too, after she was suited up. Her gaze, lingering on Ted's torso, had a lip-smacking quality to it. I couldn't blame her.

"I've got some work to do," I said, trying to sound brisk instead of forlorn. "See you, Delores."

She nodded absently and headed for the changing room. I went out the gates and back through the Magic Forest, to join Drake.

29

HE was sitting in his car, his fingers tapping impatiently on the steering wheel. One of those fancy minivans hovered in the street behind him, ready to take his spot; things are busy there by the Magic Forest. Another car started up, and the harassed-looking woman driving the minivan looked undecided. Drake solved her dilemma by barely waiting for me to get in the car before he pulled away from the curb. "So what took you so long? Were you comparing hairstyles or something?"

"I have no hairstyle," I said, in the grip of a deep inferiority complex. It's not that I want to be like Delores Mitchell, but somehow her perfection always calls my own femininity into question. Especially since I've been repressing it for years. "You didn't tell me you'd interviewed her already. What were the terms of the reverse mortgage?"

"The savings and loan has a lien on her house," he said, after a moment of silence. "They did advance her money,

146

but it was very recently. Chances are she didn't have time to use it. In these cases, the house is usually sold to pay off the savings and loan. Anything left is distributed according to the homeowner's will." He frowned, and spoke partly to himself. "Mitchell didn't know who benefited under the will, but she did say she'd been very close to Vivien—gave her a lot of help with her finances, which were evidently very tangled."

"She has a group of people at the Senior Center who sing her praises night and day." I tried to keep my voice from showing what I thought about this. "So Vivien was having money trouble? She didn't say anything about it to me, but of course I couldn't have done anything to help. She was very careful about groceries, I know." I looked out the windshield. "This isn't the way to Claudia's house."

"I've got to swing by my place and pick up some papers that I hope I left there." Drake glanced quickly at me. "It won't take more than a minute. Will Claudia worry?"

"I can't imagine her doing so. I left her a note, in any case."

Drake's trailer park was off El Camino in south Palo Alto—one of the few trailer parks allowed in the city, and only because it had been there forever. I had cruised through it a couple of times, wondering if I could swing the rental on a space, find a way to buy a trailer—but it was as far out of my reach as a mansion in Atherton.

The trailers were old, for the most part, some with flower boxes edging their parking spaces. The one Drake pulled up in front of had a straggling pot of marigolds next to the door. His trailer looked like about a thirty-footer, ten wide. He didn't invite me inside. I waited in the car, mentally pinching back the marigolds and installing a new screen door in place of the badly sagging aluminum one. Looking at it reminded me that I needed to lube the door on my bus and fix up a few things. Old buses need constant maintenance or they start to decompose. I couldn't afford to let that happen. In the best of cases, if I managed to scrape through this whole thing, I might come out with a little money, thanks to Vivien, bless her kind heart. But that same money could spell my doom, since it was the only motive around if Vivien's death were foul play. I would be lucky to be able to take to the road again in my bus. Fixing the door was like crossing my fingers, a hopeful sign that all would be well.

The trailer park was quiet, with the distant sound of dryers tumbling clothes from the cinderblock utility area. Another car drove slowly past, and I wrote the driver off as someone like me, checking out the feasibility of finding a cheap place to live in Palo Alto. It was a rental car, shiny and out of place in the well-worn ambience of the trailer park. Going past Drake's trailer, the car slowed even more, and I wondered if it was someone who knew Drake and wanted to see what woman occupied his front seat. I shrank down, turning my head away. The car speeded up, bouncing through the potholes on its way out.

Drake's Saab grew stuffy. I wanted to get back to Claudia's. She might wake up and worry about me despite my note. This was a new concern for me—that someone might be benevolently interested in my movements. I got out, crunching over the gravel to the trailer door. Inside there was a sound of drawers banging and muffled cursing. I stopped just inside the door, looking around.

The place was in a hurricane state, as if the cops who'd searched my bus had a regular gig here. Aside from the clutter, it was like no other trailer I'd ever seen, and I'd lived in a few. The kitchen was clean, but instead of the standard plywood cabinets, it had been lined with shelves displaying an incredible assortment of cookware—woks, copper pans and molds, baking pans ranging from rectangular bread pans to an angel food cake pan, mixing bowls large and small, and a pegboard crowded with arcane utensils. Instead of the standard Formica-topped dinette table and matching chairs, there was a butcher block table whose scarred maple bore testimony to its usefulness, and an assortment of ancient wooden chairs. A few snapshots were displayed on the refrigerator—a couple of children grinning toothless grins, a willowy woman holding up a cake decorated to resemble the *Los Angeles Times* and bearing the inscription "Good Luck Signe," and one of Bridget standing beside her Suburban, hugely pregnant and not looking too pleased to be photographed that way.

Drake came storming out of the back of the trailer and caught me looking at the last photo. "Some pinup, huh?" He scowled, whether at me or the photo I didn't know. "Did you get tired of waiting?"

"Yup." I looked at the living room space, maybe ten feet square and crowded with bookshelves and a couple of beanbag chairs. A TV cart under the window held a small TV and VCR, nearly obscured by overflowing stacks of videotapes. "Do much entertaining?"

"Sure. Parties every night." He began to hunt through the mound of papers on the bookshelf nearest the door. I thought that his trailer was as solitary and self-contained as my bus, though he had the advantage in space. Presumably there was even a bedroom and a bathroom beyond the living room. I was especially interested in the bathroom, but somehow couldn't find words to indicate that.

"What are you looking for?" I said instead.

"File folder." He still pawed at a miscellaneous heap of unopened mail and magazines. "Brought it home two days ago to look over, and haven't seen it since." He did glance up then, briefly. "Listing of all the deaths in the area, suspicious or not."

I wandered around the bookshelves, digesting this. "So you were already looking for more murders disguised as old people dying. You didn't need Ramsey to point it out to you."

He grabbed a likely looking folder from the bottom of a pile. It turned out to be an envelope, not what he wanted. The pile teetered ominously. "Kind of thing us trained detectives are supposed to do," he mentioned, shoving the pile back against the wall.

'Cruising the books, I noticed a large proportion of poetry and philosophy, with a smattering of biography. Near the floor beside one of the beanbag chairs was a shelf of well-thumbed murder mysteries. I pushed the chair aside to get a better look, and saw the edge of a file folder peeking out. "Is this what you were looking for?"

He grabbed it, flipping through the few pieces of paper it contained. "That's it. Thanks. Not that this helps much, but we have to rule things out."

"Can we go now? I want to get back to Claudia's."

He shuffled his feet a little. "I was going to offer you a cup of tea. I made scones last night, and they turned out well."

I hesitated, sensing a trap of some kind. The invitation might mean a change in our relationship from hunter and hunted to that of social near-equals. Or else I was meant to think that it would.

Either way, it was a change—and one I had a choice about. I do not voluntarily seek change; it's usually forced on me by circumstance. The counselor I'd seen briefly when I'd filed for divorce told me I was too passive in my approach to life. Perhaps that's true. After thinking about it, though I decided I was not so much being passive as seeking to camouflage myself, hiding as a threatened animal will. The animal's choice is between passivity and death. For many years, I'd seen this as my only option, too.

Now I had to face the notion that passivity would no longer save me. It was time to make changes; I could change my relationship with Paul Drake, or I could back away and maintain the strained distance between us.

My inability to choose was a choice in itself. Drake put the folder down on the table and turned toward the stove. "I'll start the water," he said. "Bathroom's that way, phone's this way. Help yourself to either."

At least I had no difficulty making this choice. The bathroom was small, but there was a tub that would be just the right size for a short person—like me. The fixtures were the original ones, and could have used some caulk in strategic places. Turquoise had been a popular color when the trailer was built, but it wasn't so attractive when discolored by age and hard water. I snooped through the medicine cabinet on general principles, but didn't even find a box of Trojans—nothing but shaving cream, razor, toothbrush, and several different kinds of headache medicine.

Drake was pouring water into two mugs. There was a plate of scones on the table. I sat down at one end, and he put a mug in front of me.

"So what does this mean?" I dunked the tea bag up and down. Good Earth cinnamon—a little heavy on the flavor for my taste, but better than Red Zinger. "You're breaking bread with the suspect. Can it be that you don't suspect me anymore?"

"That's a possibility." He had his glasses back on, and with them his inscrutability. "Or else I'm planning to soften you up so I can extract more juice from you."

"Sounds painful." The aroma of the cinnamon should have been pleasant and relaxing, but it was too strong. I fished the tea bag out and Drake pushed an empty saucer over to me.

"Have a scone." He offered me one, and bit into his with obvious relish. The scone was dense but light, rich-tasting, studded with tiny currants.

"You're a good baker." Whether it was the disarming quality of eating a policeman's homemade treats, or delayed reaction from my swim, I felt much more relaxed. "I believe I'm softened up now."

"Okay." He reached behind him and yanked a small tape recorder off one of the shelves. My sense of relaxation seeped away, replaced by tension. He put the tape recorder on the table between us, told it my name and the date, and then asked me "Are you aware that this conversation is being taped?"

"Yes." My lips didn't want to move, but at least it was better than being in that tiny cubicle at the police station, with the wheels of Justice grinding away visibly.

"Is this okay with you?" He nodded, prompting me to reply in the affirmative. I said yes. The switch was within my reach. If I didn't like the way it was going, I would turn off the tape recorder, walk out of the kitchen, away from my half-eaten scone and the overpowering scent of cinnamon.

"This conversation relates to the deaths of Eunice Giacometti and Vivian Greely, which may link with the homicide investigation of Gordon Murphy and Alonso Beaudray," he intoned. "You are at liberty to refuse to answer any question that you feel may incriminate you. By consenting to this taped conversation, you have waived the right to have an attorney present. This conversation will be considered admissible as evidence in a court of law. Do you understand that, Ms. Sullivan?"

I felt like turning the damned thing off then and there. But after all, I wanted the truth about these deaths as much as anyone. "I wasn't aware of it until you said so, Detective Drake," I barked into the tape recorder.

He turned the tape off and glared at me. "This is just the legal mumbo-jumbo I have to go through. Do you want to do this or not?"

"I don't want to," I said, crossing my arms over my chest. "But I will, if you'll cut the cackle. How come you weren't taping at Claudia's?"

"There was a witness there. This is my witness now." He turned the tape recorder back on. "Tell me about your relationship with these two women."

Haltingly at first, until I got into the monologue, I recounted the story of my writing workshop, summarized the personalities of Carlotta and the other ladies, and, at Drake's request, described the stories Eunice and Vivien had written. I recounted everything I'd known or heard about each woman's private life, down to Vivien's love of sweets and the ridiculous feud between her and Carlotta over the retirement home. He asked about surviving relatives and I dredged up what I knew. Vivien had none. Eunice had a niece somewhere, but I thought I'd heard that the niece was mentally incompetent. Both of them had lived frugally on limited incomes, taking full advantage of the services the Senior Center provided. Both of them owned old houses free and clear, but had trouble with upkeep. Both had been approached by Ted Ramsey to sell to him for his new condo project. Both had elected to take out reverse mortgages with Federated Savings and Loan. And, it transpired, Eunice had been found in similar circumstances to Vivien, but after a couple of days had passed. Nothing in her death had seemed inconsistent with natural causes, but no one had thought to look for suspicious circumstances then.

That was all I knew about any parallels between them. I hadn't known Eunice as well as Vivien. And I hadn't been intimate with Vivien. We were friends, we talked mostly about writing, I did a few little things for her. What I knew about her wouldn't be helpful to the police—the fine tremor in her thin hands when she cut slices of that cake she loved, her sweet tooth, her love of flowers and bright colors, the quiet way she had of seeing into people. She hadn't judged or laughed at the foibles she uncovered—she simply used them to enrich her writing. More and more, I understood how I would miss her.

All this took only half an hour, though when it was over I felt wrung out. Drake had made notes while I talked and he questioned. He looked at them thoughtfully, his eyebrows pulled down over those blank glasses. Then he pushed back his chair.

"You've been very helpful." He looked down at me and reached out a hand. I let him pull me to my feet, and I didn't snatch my hand away afterward. Not for a couple of seconds, anyway. I could feel his eyes on my mouth. He rubbed one finger along my lower lip. "A little piece of currant stuck there." His voice was gruffer. I jerked my hand free and turned toward the door.

He took the hint. There was nothing personal in the way he opened the car door for me, shut me in as if he was shutting a cell after me. While he walked around the car I stared out my window, my head averted from the driver's seat. The neighbor next to Drake's had a big jack-o'-lantern on the stoop in front. A witch with accordion-pleated arms and legs hung from the door, jerking in a most realistic way when the wind blew, as if she'd been hung. The wind was cold, the sky was cold, and my arms were cold, even though I hugged them to my chest in the defensive posture that signals, so the counselor had told me, low self-esteem. At that moment, it seemed like the least of my problems.

30

BRIDGET'S huge car was in Claudia's driveway when Drake pulled over in front of the house, muttering angrily about the tailgater who sped insolently away in his shiny new car. "Someday," Drake swore, "I'll get a new car too and brush every old heap off the road. That guy's lucky I didn't give him a ticket."

"Uh-huh." I wasn't listening. In Claudia's front yard, a dwarfish space alien grappled with a foreshortened Batman. When I got out of the car, they stopped pointing explosive fingers at each other and raced over.

"Aunt Liz. What are you going to be for Halloween?"

That was Corky. He pushed back the Batman mask and grinned at me, showing a big hole in his smile where his front tooth used to be.

Sam, beside him, was still in character. He jumped up and down around me, chanting "Guess what I am. Guess, guess, guess."

He had a purple papier-mâché head, a bit lumpy but impressive, with a huge cyclops eye painted in the center of what would have been the face, and a glitter-covered horn protruding from the forehead. His four-year-old body was swathed in purple long johns, purple turtleneck, and purple cape made from fake fur.

"Gosh, that's hard." I took a step back and bumped into Drake, who'd climbed out of the car and stood behind me.

"He's a one-eyed, one-horned, flying purple people-eater," Corky said impatiently. "That's so lame."

"Is not lame." Sam turned on his brother. "I'm going to eat you next!"

"Great outfits, fellows." Drake stepped forward and examined Batman's utility belt, which clanked with a number of implements not commonly found around a six-year-old's waist. I especially liked the bar strainer. "Who's your *costumier*?"

Bridget appeared in the front door. "I wondered who was out here. You boys were supposed to be playing in the backyard."

"One of those old rose bushes grabbed my cape," Batman complained. "And Sam keeps trying to get my utility belt off."

"You should take off the costumes now." Bridget waved us up the walk. "We'll go home in just a minute. You don't want to mess them up before tonight."

"Trick or treat tonight!" Both boys forgot their grievances and danced around the front yard in a frenzy of anticipated pleasure.

"Candy, candy, candy!" Sam's chant came out slightly muffled from his papier-mâché head, and Corky's implements clanked.

"I'm going to every house for miles!" Corky ran up and down the sidewalk. "I'm going to get ten pounds of candy!"

"We definitely need some quiet time here," Bridget said, shaking her head. "Thank God Halloween only comes once a year."

Claudia was sitting at the kitchen table, the inevitable pile of rough draft in front of her. "Sounded like some kind of Druid rite going on out there," she remarked. "Did you have a nice swim, Liz?"

"The swim was relaxing," I said. Drake was watching Bridget, who had slung her bag over her shoulder and was hunting around the kitchen for something. Suddenly he turned to look at me, and I dropped my eyes quickly.

"Here it is." Bridget found a small knapsack under one of the kitchen chairs. "What with parties at school today, and then all the candy tonight, these guys are going to be zombies tomorrow. Halloween at least falls on Friday this year."

"That's right. I meant to get some candy," Claudia said.

"We'll give any trick-or-treaters what's left of the doughnuts." I saw that the box was still on the table.

Bridget shook her head. "Never give out something like that," she said seriously. "The parents will just throw it away. You only give trick-or-treaters wrapped stuff from the store. Even that isn't safe from tampering, but it's more likely to be."

"I thought no one went door to door anymore on Halloween." Drake was investigating the doughnut box. "Heard it was all parties now."

"We go out." Bridget shrugged. "We go to houses of people we know, or whom we know have children. The boys really love it." Loud shrieks from the front yard underlined her words. "I'd better go. I have to pick up Mick at Melanie's, and Moira at Pam's." She hugged me, and patted Claudia's arm. "You're just about back to normal, aren't you?"

I glanced sharply at my hostess. Once her ankle was better, I would have no reason to stay around.

"It still gives me trouble," Claudia admitted grudgingly. "I can't carry anything or it really hurts." She turned to me. "Tomorrow afternoon," she said sternly, "we must get to the roses. If that's all right with you."

"Fine." If Claudia wanted to pretend she still needed me to hang around, I would pretend, too. The thought of being on my own again was too frightening, which was itself paralyzing. Was I going to lose my ability to make it in the world on my own? I didn't want to start having to depend on people.

Claudia limped down the hall with Bridget. Drake shut

the doughnut box and looked at me. "So you're going to be staying for a while."

"Looks that way." I shrugged.

"That's good. If you left here, you'd have to go to the Carver Arms or somewhere where we could keep track of you."

"Like jail?" I made my voice light, but Drake didn't smile.

"That might be best," he muttered. "I'm taking a real risk on you."

"Thank you so much." I straightened the edges of Claudia's manuscript, waiting for Drake to leave.

He came to stand beside me. "You would be a lot safer in jail," he said, putting one hand on my arm. "I know you're not going to do the fugitive thing, but someone just might be successful at killing you if I let you run around."

"No one will kill me." I shrugged off his hand. "I'm the scapegoat here."

Claudia came back down the hall, carrying a small box in her hand. "Talk about providential," she gloated. "Someone came by selling candy just after Bridget left. Now we're fixed for Halloween."

I reached for the box, but Drake was before me. He whipped it out of Claudia's hands and used a dishtowel to protect the lid when he lifted it off. We all looked inside. Rows of normal-looking chocolate-covered almond clusters filled the box, just as the lid said.

"You couldn't hand these out," Drake said after a moment. "They're not individually wrapped." He looked at Claudia. "Who was selling them?"

"Some little school kid." Claudia sounded defensive. "Raising money for a class trip to Hawaii, I think she said."

Drake took a pencil off the table and poked delicately at the line of chocolates. "This is the oldest, most hackneyed thing in the book," he muttered.

"You think they're poisoned." Claudia looked pleased. "Just like Miss Silver."

"Damn it, every one of you is making light of this,"

Drake exploded. "People have died, and may still. I'll have to go check up on this kid. Which way did she go?"

Claudia told him. Drake wrapped the dishtowel around the chocolate box and put the whole thing in a plastic bag. "I want both of you to stay the hell out of it. Close the door, turn out the porch light, let Halloween pass you by. I'll come back with a pizza for dinner, and I'll be checking in regularly before then. I want to speak with each of you when I do. Do you understand?

"Really, Detective—"

"No excuses." He turned at the front door. "Once again, lock everything."

After he was gone, Claudia and I looked at each other, and I locked the front door. "Masterful," was all she said.

31

CLAUDIA spent the rest of the afternoon in her study, transcribing old diaries. I went over some of my notes for the *Smithsonian* article, but I couldn't settle. A deep-seated restlessness set me to cleaning out the cupboards in Claudia's kitchen. Since I wouldn't be around forever, I wanted to leave the place in good condition. I found ancient tubes of cake-decorating frosting, a box of baking soda hardened into a ghostly brick, an epoxy-like stain where a bottle of molasses and a box of oregano had evidently collided, and an assortment of dusty jars filled with someone's abandoned health-food grains. One of the drawers was crammed with junk mail dated as long ago as 1968. Shoved way in the back of a corner cupboard was a huge box of balloons of various sizes, sprinkled with stars and musical notes. I blew one up; it didn't explode. Behind the balloons was a cheerleader's megaphone, its vinyl trim peeling.

When Claudia came out for some tea, I showed her my finds. She stared fixedly at them for a moment.

"Carlie's megaphone," she said softly. "Her senior year in high school. And the balloons—they were for Jack's twenty-first birthday." She batted at the star-covered one I'd blown up. "He's pushing thirty now. I remember I was going to put up balloons and confetti everywhere, but his friends had different ideas about decorating." She picked up a couple of the balloons, turning them to let the silvery stars catch the light.

"We could put the box on the front step for the trick-or-treaters to help themselves." I had never met Claudia's kids, of course. Bridget had mentioned that the daughter was a TV producer who lived in New York; she came home for major holidays. The son lived in the Midwest and visited rarely. Claudia went back to see him once in a while, but he'd turned into a Republican and his wife was opposed to offering hospitality to anyone, especially relatives.

Claudia shook herself out of her mood. "Good idea." She stuffed the balloons she held absently into the pocket of her sweater. "Why on earth are you wasting your time cleaning? Get back to your writing." She glared at me and stumped away to her study, carrying an enormous mug of tea.

She was right, but I knew I couldn't write with such an unsettled churning going on inside me. At least the cabinets were clean. I took three bags of trash out to the garbage cans, and went to potter around in the greenhouse. If we were going to plant seeds from the rose hips the next day, we would need to soak them overnight. I found some plastic cups and used a marker to write on them, according to the labels on the hips, before I filled them with water.

The flesh of the hips was gooshy around the knobby seeds; I broke them open one at a time, gently, and emptied

159

the seeds of each into its cup. If the seeds floated, they were no good.

A person could spend a good deal of time in garden work and never get tired of it. I thought about my vegetable plot, how I needed to go and harvest the rest of the beets, check the brussels sprouts and broccoli seedlings, clean up and mulch for the coming winter rains. Such thoughts were soothing; they implied that I would be free to garden, that the planet would continue without blowing up, that global warming would not impact the climates, and that Gaia would prevail over the dark forces lined up against her. I pictured the world goddess overthrowing industrialism as I worked though the rose hips. The greenhouse smelled of leaf mold and potting soil. It was cold, with occasional scurries of wind blowing through the broken pane in the roof, riffling the old paper seed packets that littered the workbench. Faintly from the tall trees at the back of Claudia's property came the tapping of branches against each other, or a woodpecker decimating the bug population.

The sun went behind a cloud. It was getting late; soon Drake would show up with his pizza. Stretching, I walked out of the greenhouse, shutting the door so the wind wouldn't turn over my plastic cups and mix all the seeds up.

The tapping was louder, oddly rhythmical for a bird. Something about it caught my attention, and I realized that it wasn't a woodpecker. It was a typewriter, being used by someone unaccustomed to it. The sound could have come from another writer on the block behind Claudia's, but it was too immediate for that, and too recognizable, somehow, but skewed, as your own face is in a photograph. After all, I'm probably the last writer in the Silicon Valley to use a typewriter. And that was mine I heard, clacking away, the sound familiar but the rhythm ragged. Coming from my bus, parked behind Claudia's garage.

I thought about going for help, but if I did, the intruder might get away before I could return. The anger that had alternated with fright for the past few days rushed to the surface, a geyser ready to erupt. It was so unfair that I, who had little more than my vehicle and typewriter, should have those things be as threatened as was my freedom to use them.

And more than anything, I had to know who was doing this. I had to know if it was Tony. Somehow it was like him to invade my space, try to take over the means of livelihood I'd found.

The fence behind the garage that marked the boundary of Claudia's yard was missing a board here and there; it would have been no big task to get into the bus without coming up the driveway. If this was the same person who'd hid those mysterious seeds in my little fridge, he must have known how noisy it was to crunch along that gravel, right past the house windows.

I knew how noisy it was, too. I crept around the other side of the garage, dodging as best I could the blackberry brambles that shrouded it. They made good cover, though. I crouched behind them, snagging my old sweater badly, and looked around the corner.

I was too low to see through the windows. The side door was closed, but the cardboard that had blocked off the broken window now hung down from it, dangling remnants of duct tape. The clacking of typewriter keys sounded louder. It was definitely coming from inside the bus.

Straightening a little, I tried to see inside, but the slowly gathering darkness made the interior so shadowy and vague that I couldn't tell if what I saw was a seat back or a person. Then the typing stopped, followed by the ratcheting sound of paper being pulled out of the platen, accompanied by a muffled curse.

So my phantom writer was having trouble. I would have been sympathetic under other circumstances.

The platen rolled again, and the typing started up again. It's always harder to see into a car than to see out of it; inside the bus it was probably still pretty light, and black print on a white page has its own luminescence. I would have to get right up to the window to see who it was in there, sweating over composition. Other people's cars were broken into so their radios could be stolen; mine was broken into by someone who really needed to write. I tried to tell myself it was highly entertaining, but the hair had already lifted on the back of my neck.

I looked around for a handy weapon, but assault rifles don't grow on blackberry bushes, although reading the newspaper sometimes you might think differently. All I had was the pocket knife I had just been using to split rose hips with.

Holding it opened to the biggest blade, I crept closer to the bus, debating whether to go around to the fence side, where the person couldn't easily get at me if I were discovered, but where I would be trapped if guns were the order of the day, or just to peer in through the windshield and hope to be able to see enough.

In the end, that was the simplest thing to do, so I did it.

The interior of the bus looked so much darker than the overcast dusk that spread around me. At the center of that darkness, hovering over my typewriter on the pull-up table, was something even blacker, a huge shape that I couldn't relate to anyone I knew, not even Tony. Then the typing stopped again, and a hand, a pale glimmer, came out of the blackness to rip the paper from the platen. It's not the best thing for a typewriter, but I didn't even wince.

"Damn it." The words came out strangely muffled. Then the pale hands moved up and I thought, Whatever it is, it's going to tear its hair in frustration. There was upheaval, and suddenly a face emerged from the darkness as an oval whiteness. The eyes were looking straight at me.

I ducked, and spent a moment dithering about my escape route—around to the side and through the space in the fence where two boards were gone? That was the way the intruder had come, I was sure. I didn't know if I wanted to risk that, and it left Claudia unprotected until I could race around the block and get to the phone.

On the other hand, I sure wasn't going past the door of the bus. I could hear it opening, so I started back the way

I'd come, through the blackberries to the garage, still clutching my open knife in my hand.

"Wait!"

The voice stopped me cold. It wasn't Tony's. It was a woman's.

I turned, astounded, and nearly screamed. Pursuing me was a grotesque black creature with a human head. At least, that's how it looked for the two seconds it took me to recognize what it was. Certainly it was the last person I would have expected to see dressed up in a gorilla suit.

"What on earth are you doing?" I stood there, gaping at her, while she closed the distance between us with a couple of long strides. The running shoes she wore didn't really go with the gorilla outfit.

"What are you doing with that knife?" She sounded accusing, as though I was the one acting weird. I glanced stupidly down at my hand, and she reached out and plucked the knife away from me, smiling sweetly. Then she gestured with it toward the door of the bus. "Come on."

"Why? Where?" I backed away a little, and her smile vanished.

"Stop it," Delores Mitchell said. "I don't want to have to hit you on the head again." She pointed with the knife once more, and I debated just running away, escaping this lunatic. "Don't try to run," she said, when I backed farther away. "I have a gun, too, and I don't mind using it to kill you and that ugly old woman."

The threat to Claudia stopped me, and Delores put her head to one side, the smile returning. "So you don't want to be shot? I don't blame you." She shuddered. "It needn't come to that. Get into that wretched vehicle, and we'll talk."

I wasn't really frightened of her—after all, though she was taller than me and probably as aerobically toned as possible, I was pretty scrappy myself. She tossed the knife into the air and caught it as it flashed down in the feeble light—by the blade. "I know how to throw knives," she

163

said in her light, somewhat prissy voice. "If you run, I'll spit you like a chicken."

I got into the bus. It seemed like the thing to do. And I was extremely curious, especially when I saw the head of the gorilla costume on the bench seat.

Delores stood at the side of the bus, blocking the open doorway. She should have looked ridiculous, her body smothered in the gorilla suit, her head and hands free. Her hands, I noticed, were encased in surgical gloves. She didn't look that funny to me.

32

I sat on the bench seat of the bus, feeling totally confused. The surgical gloves, the gorilla costume—"Just what's going on, Delores?"

"I don't understand why they haven't arrested you yet." She sounded angry. "You're the obvious suspect in every case."

"Just lucky, I guess." I stared at her curiously. Even without the prim suits and the fancy shoes, Delores still looked incredibly clean-cut. "Are you going to a costume party somewhere, is that it? And you needed to dash off a sonnet or something on the way so you just broke into my bus to use the typewriter—"

"You don't have a clue," she said impatiently. "I should have stuck to my original plan, but—" She gazed into space for a moment. Her usually sleek hair was disheveled by the gorilla head; still wearing those surgical gloves, she began to pat and smooth it. "This is better," she decided at last. "Since you're here, you can type the note."

"What note?" I used the soothing voice recommended when speaking to those who have lost touch with reality. The incongruity of her costume didn't diminish Delores' perkiness a jot. The effect should have been amusing, but it was exceedingly creepy instead. She closed my knife with a decisive click, but she didn't give it back. Instead she pulled a gun from somewhere in her hairy gorilla flank and pointed it at me. An immediate adrenaline jolt reverberated though all my nerve endings.

"I'm a very good shot." Her hand was certainly steady on the gun. "Daddy always believed it was important for a woman to be able to defend herself. He taught me to throw knives and hunt and target-shoot. I've never shot a person yet, but it might be kind of exciting—different from the paper target, you know."

"I don't imagine your dad had this sort of thing in mind," I said, casting around for something that might improve the situation. My mind didn't want to believe that this was happening, but my body was buying it; the words that came out of my mouth were shaky. "What will he think when you get arrested?"

"He died last year." Delores's lower lip quivered. "I really miss him, but it would be selfish to want him alive when he was in such bad shape." She sniffed. "It was for his sake, really. That's when I found out how easy it was."

It took a moment before her words sank in. "You mean you—you killed your dad?"

"I didn't kill him," she protested. "He was very sick. He was dying anyway." Her face changed, looked younger. "It was just him and me for so long, after Mummy died," she murmured, almost crooning. "He used to call me DoDo—he used to like me to wear her dresses. A man has needs, you know." She blinked, but the febrile glitter in her eyes didn't dissipate. "After he got sick he didn't want DoDo anymore. He was just a sick old man. He wanted to die. They all wanted to die." Her grip on the gun tightened. "I don't know why I'm telling you this. But it's safe, because you're going to die, too."

"I don't—" I had difficulty getting the words past the dryness in my throat. "I don't want to die, Delores."

"You have to," she said matter-of-factly. "When you're dead, everything will be settled."

"No, it won't." I didn't know if trying to be logical with someone whose sanity was slipping away would work. "Another death will just raise more questions. Your dad would have known that. He wouldn't want you to keep killing people."

She wasn't really listening. "I saved all his things. This was his gun." Her voice hardened. "And he wouldn't have cared at all about someone like you. He wanted me to be happy."

"You don't need to shoot me. If you need something typed to be happy, I'll do it for you." Delores, in her bulky costume, filled the side door space; I couldn't get past her. It would be difficult to race around the table and through the passenger door before she potted me, if she meant to. I was effectively trapped. "Just tell me what you want." I pulled the typewriter toward me. The light had grown too dim; I couldn't see the words on the paper in the machine.

"Your confession, of course." Delores's gloved fingers rubbed the gun in an absent caress. I couldn't take my eyes off the gun; it looked similar to the one I had shot Tony with. At the time, I'd thought I'd rather die than shoot someone again. Now I wasn't so sure.

"Put it in your own words," Delores ordered. "On a fresh sheet of paper—how sorry you are for all the murders."

I gripped the smooth metal sides of the typewriter to keep my hands from shaking. "I didn't do the murders, Delores."

"You had opportunity, and you're obviously not . . ."—she hesitated, and I thought wildly that she didn't want to hurt my feelings—"you're not a responsible person. You don't have a house or anything but this junk heap." She flicked a disparaging glance at the interior of the bus, and I saw it for a moment through her eyes—the duct tape that mended the bench seat's upholstery, the broken window, the faded curtains.

"Maybe," I said, keeping a firm grip on both temper and sanity. "But I still didn't kill anyone."

"How can they let you go free after all the evidence against you? Those yew seeds should have convinced them."

"Yew seeds?" I must have looked too interested. She waved the gun in my face. I jerked back on the bench, and then tried to look relaxed when every muscle in my body ached with fear. "You put them in my cooler?"

"I should have taken you out then," she said, scowling at me as if we were discussing nothing more important than me stealing her lane at the swimming pool. "Actually, I thought you might be dead, and that wouldn't have suited me too well, because it might have gotten you off the hook. But this plan," she concluded with satisfaction, "is bound to work. Write the note."

"Now?" I needed time. Somewhere back in my mind was the knowledge that Drake was coming, if I could only buy enough time. Her face was just a pale circle above the blackness of her costume. The evening was still in the deep blue stage, before absolute night.

"You can turn on the light. That way I can be sure what you're doing."

"I don't need the light." I felt in the cupboard below the table where I keep copy paper. I put it in the machine, moving by touch, and then stopped helplessly.

"Just write that you murdered all of them, you're sorry, and you're taking this way out." Delores rattled it off with the self-possession of the truly poised. "I tried to do it but I kept making mistakes, and everybody knows about your boring perfect typing. Typewriters are so primitive." I could hear the disdain in her voice. "But the police could tell if the note wasn't written on this typewriter, so I had to do it this way."

I hit the return lever a couple of times, stalling. "Why the gorilla outfit, anyway?"

"It's Halloween," Delores said reasonably. "With the head on, nobody can tell if I'm a man or a woman—and no one I know would ever believe it's me in this outfit." She laughed her girlish laugh. It gave me the horrors. "When I'm through here I'll just go back to my car and take it off. I have my real costume underneath—a very nice Tahitian sarong. I am going to a party later, as a matter of fact. With Ted," she added.

"That's nice." My fingers were icy. They didn't feel strong enough to pound the keys.

"Glad you think so." Her voice roughened. "He's said a couple of times lately that he couldn't believe you would have anything to do with the deaths. That just made me so mad."

"It's the truth." I forced my hands to unclench, and tried to steady them.

"Not after tonight." Delores was openly gloating. "Ted'll have to admit he was wrong. Maybe then he'll be a little more forthcoming. Maybe when I give him the development rights to my new properties, he'll see what a good partnership we could have."

"You're going into partnership with him?" I moved my fingers onto the home row and felt the comforting cold smoothness of the keys. There was a little chip on the *f* key—my left index fingertip found it automatically.

"He should have offered it months ago; I told him I was interested." She laughed scornfully. "He thought I was just interested in him, and of course I am, but I wanted to work with him. There's real money in development if you do it right. Especially if the land costs next to nothing." She waved the gun again, and its shiny metal caught what little light there was. Again it commanded my gaze. It was an effort to look away. "Type," Delores ordered.

I typed: "Paul. Delores Mitchell is holding me at gunpoint." As a sentence, it lacked credibility. If he ever saw it, he wouldn't believe it. I kept trying to find an escape somewhere, but my brain wouldn't work at it. All it would do was embrace the cold breath of the breeze and

168

the sharp scent of Claudia's compost pile, along with the sophisticated perfume smell that was coming from Delores and the way the crows flew around the black treetops like upward-blowing leaves, cawing out their evening roost song. These would be my last sights, sounds, smells. Like Pigpen, like Vivien, I would be dead, and the world would continue on without me.

"Why?" I turned to look at the dark shape of her. "Why did I kill them?"

"Well—because." She hesitated. "You're mentally unbalanced. You hated Pigpen because he was a bum, and you hated poor Vivien because she had a house and you didn't."

"Not very good reasons." I noticed that she'd called Pigpen by his nickname. In the news reports he'd been Gordon Murphy. "Why did you kill them?"

She didn't answer for a moment. "Do you have a tape recorder on?" Leaning through the side door, she reached up and switched on the dome light. "Of course you don't—you don't have anything. I can tell you, I guess, since you're so curious. That's funny," she remarked. "I wouldn't think a person on the verge of death would be curious."

"It doesn't seem fair to die without knowing why." I didn't voice the thought that the others had died that way. In the dim light, Delores's face looked much the same—self-absorbed, self-important.

"It was Eunice's fault, really," Delores said, shifting the blame. "She asked me about reverse mortgages, if our institution had them. And we didn't. But I thought I could help her out, put some of my capital into her place, just like a reverse mortgage but private, you see." She sighed. "She had that oversized lot—the possibilities were endless. So after I saw her with those sample cereals on her counter, I got the idea, and I just couldn't wait any longer. Vivien had already approached me about a reverse for her house, and I knew with those two big parcels I could do quite a deal."

"So you killed Eunice. To get your hands on her property. Did she make you her heir?"

"Of course not." Delores sounded shocked. "That would

have been improper, and besides, it might have made me look suspicious. I have a lien on her house, and I'll just sell it to myself to pay off the costs."

"Convenient." I felt choked by the lump in my throat—of tears, of rage, of fear.

"It was fair," Delores protested. "She got the money, after all."

"But not time to spend it." I didn't mean to say the words. They just slipped out. A wave of crimson washed over Delores's face.

"She was a sick old woman whose life was a burden to her," she spat. "Now type."

I added another sentence. "She killed Eunice and Vivien—those reverse mortgages are phony." Now that the light was on, I could see that I'd misspelled "holding"—it read "hilding." But since Drake would likely never see it, the spelling didn't matter.

I had to buy more time. Swallowing my fear, I forced a casual tone. "Sounds like you planned their killings pretty well," I said. "What was it—yew seeds in the granola sample?"

"I wanted it to look like a normal death," she explained. "Or an accident or something. The seeds were hardly noticeable mixed into the cereal—and those old people don't see so well, after all. The yews grow wild on the vacant lot next to our house; I saw some program on TV about how poisonous the seeds were, so I picked the berries last summer before Daddy died." She sounded proud of her enterprise. "I mashed them through a strainer and got lots of seeds and made some tea with some of them. Daddy likes his tea with honey; he never even noticed."

"So you saved the rest of the seeds?" I needed a reality check. It was hardly believable that goody-goody Delores would say such things.

She heard my disbelief as praise for her forethought, and nodded. "I got Pigpen to collect cereal samples—told him everyone on the block had donated their samples to the Food Closet downtown. That was clever, wasn't it? He was too stupid to see through it, anyway." She looked at me, and I tried to look sympathetic. I glanced at the gun again. She was holding it in a looser grip; I wondered if I could snatch it away without horrible consequences.

"So you really fooled Pigpen." I couldn't think of anything more constructive to do than getting her to talk.

"At first." She scowled. "After Eunice died, Pigpen figured out that I was doing something illegal with the cereal samples. He tried to blackmail me!" Her voice was incredulous. "Of course I had to kill him. I gave him some tea made from the yew seeds, just like I did Daddy, just like I'm going to give you. Then I said I would drive him to the liquor store. I was going to push him into the creek, but when I saw your van parked there I knew that was better. He'd told me how you treated him. I stopped right there, whacked him on the head with my sock filled with rocks, and pushed him out. I had to get out and roll him with my foot." She wrinkled her nose in disgust. "At first I thought the smell in my car was a dead giveaway—he was so foul! I vacuumed and vacuumed, but I could still smell him until after the Beamer's weekly appointment at the Auto Laundry."

I could figure out the rest of it myself. Alonso had taken Pigpen's place, but Delores had found a real keen way of removing anyone who might connect her with cereal samples. And then Vivien, who frugally collected the free samples, quite proud of her thrift. For a moment great sadness washed the fear out of me, and then anger flooded in.

"Aren't you done yet?" Delores nudged me with the gun. "Let me see what you typed."

I gave her the paper, and reached for the gorilla head that sat on the seat beside me. Delores glanced at the first words.

"You idiot! This isn't what I asked for!" She crumpled the paper, but for a few moments it had distracted her attention.

"Neither is this." I rammed the gorilla head on backward over her head and ducked, just before she shot at me. Fire seared through my left shoulder. Before she could aim again, I managed to grab her arm above the hand that held the gun and bang it against the door frame as hard as I could. She was strong, but those little bones are delicate. The gun dropped into the grass at her feet, accompanied by her anguished cry. Then I kicked her in the stomach.

The gorilla suit provided some protection, I guess. She lurched backward, but she wasn't down. The sound of the shot should have had Claudia calling for reinforcements. I couldn't feel anything in my left shoulder except a warm trickling that was somehow reassuring. I scooted out of the bus, to where Delores was doubled up, and twisted her injured wrist as hard as I could. She screamed, and I shoved her forward. "I've got the gun now," I lied. "Just keep going straight ahead, or I'll put a bullet in you." My shoulder began to burn again; walking jarred it agonizingly. If she realized that I could barely stagger, I might yet be done for.

She cradled her wrist, whimpering. "You broke it," she whined through the gorilla head. "I can't see anything! I'm suffocating."

"Good." My anger at her was the only thing that kept me on my feet. I wanted to tear out her hair, get into a prison-quality fight with her, knock her head against the garage wall, cause her the kind of pain she'd caused Eunice and Vivien and her other victims. I wanted her to die, for a few red-eyed seconds.

The porch light over the back door hadn't gone on; I began to worry that Claudia might not have heard the shot. With her uninjured hand, Delores was trying to pull off the gorilla head. I pushed her again, and she stumbled against the garage. "Stop shoving!" She sounded really peeved at my bad manners.

"Keep going!" I wanted her far enough in front of me to be no danger, and not so far that I couldn't tackle her if need be. Not that I relished the idea of tackling. I brushed against the coil of clothesline that hung on the garage wall, and grabbed it. Delores staggered in front of me, still one-handedly pawing at her head. Closing the gap between us,

I dropped the loop of clothesline over her head. It wouldn't go past her shoulders, and she began whacking behind her with her good arm, succeeding in landing a punch on my injured shoulder.

We careened past the garage and into the backyard, Delores's costume liberally festooned with blackberry vines that had seized her fur with their thorns. I was still trying to get the rope around her to pin her arms to her sides; she was still trying to pull off the gorilla head.

Finally I remembered that I was supposed to be armed. "If you don't stand still," I ordered, "I'll just shoot you. In the other wrist."

She stood still, and I pushed the coil of rope down on one shoulder. The costume had incredibly wide shoulders—it was like dealing with a football player's uniform. And I was handicapped by the bullet wound.

Before I could shove the rope over the other shoulder, Delores tore away from me, using both her hands to wrench at the gorilla head. She was cursing and moaning with pain, and I wanted to join her in that occupation, but I had run out of adrenaline. I couldn't even move. My anger drained away, allowing the throbbing in my arm to fill me; I didn't know how to cope with the situation any longer. Delores would get the gorilla head off and see that I was unarmed and wounded, and then she'd either walk away or strangle me and walk away, and that would be that.

The gorilla head bounced on the grass, and Delores whirled wildly, catching sight of me. I had just enough fortitude left to put my hand in my pocket, pointing my finger like we used to do when playing cops and robbers. It wouldn't have fooled a sharp ten-year-old, but Delores swallowed it. She took a few steps back. "Go ahead and shoot me if you dare," she shrieked. "No one will ever believe that I killed them all. They'll think you did it and just finished up by killing me. You'll go to jail!" I winced, and she noticed that. Her voice got triumphant. "They'll probably send you to the gas chamber."

"I wouldn't shoot to kill you," I said, wiggling my finger to make my gun more convincing. "Just maim you for life."

There was a loud report, like another gunshot. A stentorian voice roared out suddenly, "Put down your weapons. The police are surrounding the house!" and there was Claudia on the back porch steps, her daughter's old cheerleading megaphone at her lips, the remains of a popped balloon dangling from her fingers.

That and the gunshot would go over big with the neighbors.

"Yeah, sure." Delores turned her head back and forth between us. "You can't stop me from leaving." She glared at Claudia. "You—you old hag!"

"So rude." The voice was Drake's. Incredibly, there he was, standing in the driveway. An officer in uniform pushed past him and then halted, puzzled, looking from me with my fake gun to Delores in her gorilla outfit, to Claudia, perched like an aging cheerleader on the back steps.

"Who do we arrest?" He was joined by another uniform, and they both looked at me—smelling the old, faint stench of my criminal record, probably.

Seeing this, Delores pointed at me. "Arrest her," she screeched. "She killed those other people, and she's threatening me with a gun. She hurt my wrist!" She held it up, and sure enough it dangled limply. "I think it's broken!"

The officers started toward me, although they were still darting glances at the gorilla suit. Drake didn't order them to back off. He did speak, however.

"Where did the gun come from?" He sounded idle, like it was just a routine question, but the uniforms halted.

"I don't—what do you mean?" Delores scowled at him. "How should I know? She probably has a whole arsenal in that junk heap of hers."

"How did she kill the others? With the same gun?"

Delores shook her head, the pretty, shiny hair swirling around her face. "She poisoned them. She gave them yew seeds and they died." Her scowl transferred itself to Claudia. "Probably got them from that woman there—there're yews on both sides of her front door."

I just stood, feeling nothing but the pain in my shoulder. The officers rushed over when I took my hand out of my pocket, surrounding me and patting me down. I didn't say anything. Who would believe me? But when they jarred my shoulder, I had to whimper.

Drake moved. "Liz. You're hurt?"

I nodded dully. "Shot—shoulder." Claudia exclaimed, and started down the stairs.

Drake stopped her. "Call the ambulance," he said curtly.

"It's on the way—should be here now." Claudia stayed on the steps, though. She must have thought the backyard looked a little crowded.

Drake came over to me, gesturing to the uniforms. They backed off until they stood on either side of Delores.

"Where's the gun?" Drake's hands moved gently over my shoulder. I wanted to be a stoic, but it was too much. I would begin crying any time. I had to breathe deeply before I could answer.

"It's somewhere back by the bus. Dropped near the side door." One of the uniforms went the direction Drake pointed. I swayed, and he put his arm around my waist, marching me over to the steps. Claudia received me, patting my back and murmuring when I sank down. A distant siren cut through the stillness.

"See, she admits it. She broke my wrist," Delores said triumphantly.

Drake nodded to the other policeman, who grasped one of Delores's hairy arms. "Like to take you in for questioning, Miss Mitchell," he said, the words polite but his voice ice-cold.

"I insist on medical care," Delores said shrilly. "I want to call my lawyer. I'll sue you for false arrest—"

"I didn't say anything about arrest yet," Drake said. "But perhaps you'd like to remove your costume? I don't want the clerk to think I've busted the circus."

175

Reluctantly, Delores accepted the uniformed cop's help unzipping the gorilla suit. The other uniform, whom I recognized as the blond surfer boy from Pigpen's death—so many eons ago—came back from behind the garage. He held a plastic bag with the gun in it, and a couple of crumpled pieces of paper. The siren was getting closer.

"Found these, too, Detective Drake." He glanced at me curiously.

"Thanks, Rucker." Drake took the paper, and with a glance at Delores's surgical gloves, smoothed it out. He looked up at me. "She's hilding you at gunpoint?" A very small smile flickered over his face.

"Everybody's a critic," I said wearily. The ambulance pulled up. The bustle they created almost drowned out Delores's outraged demands for an instant doctor. The paramedics pronounced her wrist probably broken, and Rucker scratched his head over how to handcuff her.

"You can't arrest me," she yelled. "I'm going to a Halloween party. It's all her fault—she did it. You'll look like a fool when the truth comes out."

"I don't think so." Drake spoke over his shoulder, from where he stood, hovering over me with flattering attentiveness. "You see, I'd already found out about the mortgages."

Delores shut up, like a teakettle suddenly turned off.

"What mortgages?" Claudia lost a little of her anxious look.

"Later," Drake said. "I'm taking Liz to the hospital now."

"Two visits in two days," I mumbled idiotically when he guided me to my feet. "A record."

"Just don't try to top it." He paused, looking back at Claudia. "Thanks for calling us."

"No thanks required," she said graciously. "But be sure to bring Liz back and stay to explain it all."

She stood with the megaphone at her feet, and I saw her over my shoulder as I climbed into the ambulance, where Delores sat sullenly, attended by the police. Luckily it wouldn't be a long ride.

33

"**SHE** picked on those two old women," Drake said, stretching his legs out under Claudia's kitchen table, "because they didn't have family to complicate things. She wanted their property, and figured she could get it dirt cheap because she had a lien on it. In effect, she'd sell it to herself to pay off her loan."

"I still don't understand." Claudia was stirring a pot of cocoa at the stove; the aroma of warm milk made me sleepier than I already was. I was ensconced in the rocking chair, with plenty of pillows, but I was still uncomfortable. My shoulder was stiff with bandages and my bloodstream full of painkillers. But at least I wasn't in custody. I could almost feel sorry for Delores—what lay before her was like nothing she'd ever imagined in her life.

"I mean," Claudia continued, ladling cocoa into mugs, "how could she get away with that? What about Vivien's will? Does Liz still inherit the house?"

I took the mug she handed me and waited, in a placid, drug-induced state, for Drake's answers. I was vaguely interested in them; they concerned someone I knew well.

"She could get away with it as long as there was no scrutiny," Drake said, blowing on his cocoa. It was very hot; I'd nearly scalded my tongue with my first sip. "Eunice left her property to the Senior Center, and I suppose Delores meant to give them a little money and say that was all that was left after the lien was paid off. It actually suited her to have Vivien leave her house to Liz; that made Liz look guiltier than ever. But as soon as we started looking into the finances, it all fell apart. When I spoke to Ted at the pool he was cagey, but he admitted that he'd been offered development rights to both properties since Vivien's death. He wouldn't say who offered them, but I'm sure he will now."

"So does Liz get the house?"

"Probably." Drake smiled at me, for once without that wariness I was used to seeing in him. "If she can afford to keep it."

"What does that mean?" I roused myself enough to ask the question, though my tongue felt thick and woolly.

"He means," Claudia said, pouring a little more cocoa into her mug, "that upkeep and property taxes aren't cheap around these parts. You might want to butter up Ted Ramsey."

Drake cleared his throat. "Late breaking news," he said unhappily. "The neighbors have gotten wind of Ted's project and started a major petition thing. The whole development will probably die a natural death. You could sell the house to a builder for the lot, but you don't get much for a tear-down."

"Oh well, easy come, easy go." I yawned, suddenly and hugely. "I wouldn't want to see more condos sprout up around there myself."

"There's a rental cottage behind the house, isn't there?" Claudia stirred her cocoa. "You could get some income out of it that way."

My eyes were just on the brink of closing. Drake's voice came from far away. "We can discuss this another time. Liz needs to get some rest."

"I'm all right." I pried my eyes open and smiled drowsily at both of them. "Nothing to discuss, anyway. I'll live in the cottage, rent the house."

"It's a big lot," Drake said. "You might be able to get a lot-split. You could sell one of the houses, keep the other." He started to add something, looked at my drooping eyelids, and desisted.

Sinking into the fluffy cloud that wrapped me, I knew as

well as if he'd spoken that he wanted that lot-split; he wanted to buy Vivien's house from me. It would go cheap, in the condition it was in. Such a sweetheart deal wouldn't have worked if I was dead or in the slammer, unable to profit from my supposed crimes. If I could have felt anything, I would have felt mildly disappointed.

"Liz, you're not going to make any decisions tonight." Claudia got to her feet and scowled at Drake. "You are going to bed, right now."

I stood up too, swaying only a little. "Right. My lawyers will talk to your lawyers." It sounded very grand. It would be all too easy to get used to being a person of property.

Drifting to sleep in my narrow bed, I remembered Vivien's death as something sorrowful that had happened a long time ago. Vivien and Eunice, Pigpen and Alonso. Their absence from the world had already been overwritten by what had come next. As a survivor, I was filled with rosy visions and the relaxation of tension. My shoulder would be painful, but it would heal; my life would be disrupted, but for the better. I would finally finish that article for *Smithsonian*. Vivien's house had seemed like a burden, but if I sold the house to Drake and kept the cottage, it would make all the difference. A steady income for the next few years would be like having Lady Luck hemorrhage all over me.

When I woke up, it wasn't the bright new day I'd been anticipating. Somewhere in the back of my dreaming mind was a thundering, creaking noise; when I put it together with the cold draft, I realized the window had been forced up. The curtains fluttered wildly, casting confusing shadows on the wall from the bright moonlight and bare tree branches outside. Still fuddled, I thought the gorilla suit was in the room with me, a large, dark shape creeping closer and closer.

This, I decided, was a dream, an attempt by my subconscious to begin dealing with the day's events. I kept very still and breathed very deeply, willing the dream to change into something else, willing myself to wake from it. My shoulder throbbed painfully, and then I knew I was awake. I strained my eyes in the wind-tossed moonlight, trying to tell what was shadow and what was substance.

The dark shape was substance. It was standing over me now. My hand closed around the flashlight under my pillow. I yanked it out and turned it on, suddenly.

Tony's face stared back at me, caught in the glare, blinking. Then his hand swept down, and the flashlight disappeared.

"Thanks, Liz. I needed a light." His voice was the same, smooth, caressing, with that frightening hint of violence beneath it. The flashlight came back on, aimed at me. It flicked down the length of my body, lingered on the huge, faded sweatshirt I slept in, and then came back to my face. I couldn't see behind it, but that one glimpse of Tony's face was plenty. He had changed a little, but not enough.

"You've really let yourself go, kid." He sounded amused. "You look ten years older. I wasn't even sure it was you at the swimming pool this afternoon, till I watched you walk out." He flicked the flashlight over me once more.

The swim I had wanted so badly had been my downfall, it seemed.

"Pretty smart of me, wasn't it?" The bragging note in his voice was as familiar as an old bruise, but now I could hear the insecurity beneath it. "I knew you'd turn up at that pool sooner or later. Been watching it since I got into town. Some wild party you had here tonight. I thought you and the new boyfriend were gonna be locked up, and I'd miss my chance for a little private chat."

I'd been threatened, almost killed. Ambulances, police cars—it had all looked like his kind of party to Tony.

"So," he continued after a moment. "Aren't you going to tell me how glad you are to see me? Or has the new boyfriend cut me out?"

The flashlight swung nearer, and now the violence in his voice was not just a hint. "Answer me!"

"Stop shining that light in my face." I held my voice

steady, but it was an effort. The lingering remnants of painkiller were burning off fast. My heart was pounding so hard my chest felt aflame.

He laughed and turned the flashlight off. The sudden dark was as blinding as the light had been. "Sounds like you've forgotten who gives the orders. You'll have to remember again."

I already remembered the sound of the blows, crunching inside my head, thudding into my ribs. I already remembered how the pain exploded until I wanted to die—or wanted him to.

"You don't give me orders anymore, Tony." I forced myself to sit up in the bed, thankful that my left shoulder was on the far side from Tony. When he started to hit me, I might be spared that pain at least.

He was silent for a moment. "I waited for you. Why didn't you come back? Why did you divorce me?"

"You know why." I didn't want to play this game either, the one where he was the injured party and I just got what I deserved for not being the perfect wife. "It's over, Tony. Been over for years."

He flicked the flashlight on again, moving the light until he found my face. "It's not over. You wouldn't have been hiding from me if you thought that. You wouldn't have run away if we weren't still bound together."

I wanted to deny this, but it was true that my fear and terror had dictated my life just as love and commitment do for other, luckier people. "You must leave me alone." I tried to be forcible, but I felt as if I was pinned against the wall, waiting for the pain.

Tony shook his head. "I've been looking for you for a long time, Liz. I don't believe in divorce. You're coming with me."

"No." I braced myself. "Did you ever go for counseling, like the judge said?"

"I don't need counseling." He pulled a chair forward and sat right next to the bed, still shining the light in my eyes.

"A man has a right to be with his wife. I wouldn't have had to hurt you if you'd just understood. . . ."

Understood that I was his doormat. "I wouldn't have had to shoot you if you'd just let me alone." I found myself echoing his almost regretful voice. I couldn't smell alcohol; if he wasn't drunk, he might listen to reason.

When his fist drove at me, the whisper of its movement triggered a long-buried instinct; I jerked aside. The blow fell on the wall where my head had been. Flakes of plaster rained into the bed. "Damn it!" He shook his hand. I hoped it hurt. "You should have come back, Liz, so I could've taken care of this once and for all. Now I'm really going to have to teach you a lesson."

He turned off the flashlight, set it down. Now he would beat me until I died. The unspoken words echoed between us. His blow had shaken the walls, but I couldn't count on Claudia to have noticed. She slept heavily, and her bedroom was upstairs on the other side of the house. No one would save me this time.

At least I had had security and happiness in my grasp, however ephemerally.

I was tired of being under a dark, threatening cloud all the time. I didn't want to die. But I didn't want to live on the run anymore. I didn't have the energy to fight; and blowing Tony away hadn't worked the first time. This time there was no gun to test my philosophy that I wouldn't try killing again. There was nothing left except to ask him to leave, and not to come back without an invitation. I didn't think that would work.

"You know, Tony, if you hurt me, you'll go to jail. I'll press charges, and I'll see you put away for a long time."

He laughed a little. "You may not be in any shape to talk, babe. Of course, I'll still love you when you're a vegetable, but the new boyfriend might not."

"You'll still get arrested." My eyes were getting used to the dark. I could see the white gleam of Tony's eyeballs, the pale glimmer of his shirt. I could tell he was nerving himself for the first hit, for the surge of self-justifying adrenaline that comes with it. "If you hurt me bad, if you kill me, you won't get out for a long time, Tony, because they'll bring a first-degree charge—premeditation, probably special circumstances." I spoke fast, the words tumbling out, needing to convince him. "In California, that could mean execution."

"Who's talking about killing?" He backed off a little. "I just want to teach you—show you—" The pent-up anger of years radiated from him. His hands were clenched already. "Besides, look what you tried to do to me!"

"I found something out about death recently, Tony." I didn't know how much longer I could keep him from hitting me. "Dead people have this look. Their eyes follow you. They're dead, but they don't look finished with life, somehow." He shifted his position. It was hard to hold my voice steady. "After you kill me, I'll be with you, all right. You'll see me everywhere. You'll probably be glad when they execute you."

"They won't execute me." He hissed at me, putting his face down by mine. "No one will even notice what happens to a tramp like you."

"Yes, they will." I braced my back against the wall, trying to keep my wits about me. "That new boyfriend—he's a cop, Tony. I told him all about you. He'll track you down, wherever you hide. He'll see that they throw the book at you. If you're going to kill me, you might as well kill yourself, too, right off the bat. You won't like prison. You won't like running and hiding, either. Believe me, I know."

He loomed over me, his frustration and fury tangible. I hoped I wouldn't beg for mercy, that I would endure what came with dignity. But then his hands closed around my neck, crushing painfully. I forgot about dignity. I clawed at his fingers, but he was strong.

We were face to face. My back arched, my heels dug into the bed. I could taste his sour breath, see the sheen of his eyeballs, just like Pigpen's. No, that was wrong. I would be like Pigpen, wide-eyed but dead, seeing nothing.

His hands slackened, and I could breath again. I sucked in cool gulps of air, sagging back against the wall.

The fury seemed to go out of him. Sighing, he loosed his grip.

"You always did talk too much, Liz." He picked up the flashlight, flicking it on again, then off. "I've spent years thinking about how I'd beat the shit out of you for what you did."

"Wouldn't get you anywhere." The words felt harsh, forced through my throat in a scratchy whisper.

"Yeah, yeah." He tossed the flashlight at me. It bounced off the bed onto the floor with a tiny chime of breaking glass. "You're really just a mousy, smart-mouthed female. Don't know what I saw in you in the first place." He sounded a little puzzled. "All this time I've waited, and now it doesn't seem worth it."

"Good . . . choice." I swallowed, painfully.

He stooped over me again, but then turned away. "Don't push your luck, bitch. You've already cost me too many years."

"That's funny." I watched him move toward the window, and felt suddenly an odd flicker of kinship. We had been locked together for so long by our common enmity. "I feel . . . the same."

He paused, straddling the windowsill, and I could see the cocky, swaggering spirit that had been so attractive to me once. "Tell your cop boyfriend I'm laying off," he said. "If he wants used goods, that's his loss. I've got better things to do than go after a woman who sleeps in that getup."

He swung out of the window. I heard the gravel crunch under his feet as he walked away.

The silence would have been loud if it hadn't been for the thundering of my heart. After a few minutes I struggled out of bed and shut and locked the window. Houses were just an illusion of safety, after all; one good blow and the lock wouldn't matter. I turned on the light and brushed the plaster dust out of the sheets, picked up the shards of flashlight and dumped them in the wastepaper basket. The hole wasn't too bad; after I spackled it in the morning, there'd be no evidence, nothing to show that the night's encounter had actually happened.

There was emptiness inside me, where I'd always kept my fear and anger. Tony was gone, and I hadn't had to kill him. It was more as if I had finally let him go, when his actions ceased to matter. From now on our karmic circles would be separate. My future could be a matter of choice, not reaction. His future, I hoped, would soon run smack against some well-deserved event, like crashing his motorcycle into a sturdy brick wall.

I was cold, very cold. The pan of cocoa was still in the kitchen; I crept in quietly and heated it, drawing a spoon across the top to take off the skin that had formed. The warmth felt good on my throat. I was hunched over a steaming cup when Claudia appeared in the doorway, yawning.

"I thought I heard something," she said, around another immense yawn. "Are you all right? Have a bad dream?"

"Yes." I cleared the croak out of my throat, feeling the comforting warmth of the cup between my palms. "But I don't think it will come back."

34

I was sitting on my front steps, eating an Empire apple and reading *Chronicles of Avonlea*. It was one of those early December days that are really lost bits of summer, trying to get back. The sun shone mightily, but the air held a bite, and there were clouds building in the west. I was ready for the rain; I had planted some tulips and daffodils down my tiny front walk, and could not wait for spring to come.

Drake's car pulled up behind my bus, and he came down the walk. "You painted your place."

"It wasn't hard." I put the apple core inside and shut my book. "I wanted it all sealed against the winter rains."

He stood back a little, like an art critic. "I like it," he said judiciously. I did, too. Just white paint, green shutters, the best quality I could afford. My labor had been pretty cheap, and the check from *Smithsonian* had covered the cost of the paint.

"I'll do your house for you, for a fee." I looked at him. It had been nearly a month since we'd started all the paperwork relating to our transfer of property; I had met him to sign things once in a while, but we hadn't really talked. He would be moving in soon.

"I thought you might call," he said, sitting on the step beside me. "Ask for help shingling the roof or something."

"It was no problem." I kept my voice casual.

"Humph." He reached for my book. "It would be for me." His voice changed. "*Chronicles of Avonlea?* What's this?"

"A trip down Memory Lane." I took the book away and set it inside by the apple core. Something about owning my own little place had started me reading the cozy, long-forgotten stories of my childhood. In the past couple of weeks, I had taken armloads of books out of the children's library. It was a vacation from reality; I'd enjoyed every minute of it.

Drake clearly didn't know what I was talking about, and didn't much care. "Actually," he said, reaching into the pocket of his shabby tweed jacket, "I came to drop off my first official house payment."

"Thanks." I went inside to put the envelope away, and he followed me, looking around curiously. The cottage was three rooms—small bedroom, small living room and tiny kitchen. Compact as it was, my stuff didn't begin to fill it, though just the other day I'd bought a waffle iron at a second-hand store in Redwood City for $4.50. I had

Vivien's bedroom set, and her worn couch and faded rug looked fine in the living room. I'd painted all the walls, scrubbed all the wavy glass in the windows.

"You've really been in a nesting frenzy here, haven't you?" Drake touched one of the new curtains. Vivien had also had an old Kenmore sewing machine, and I'd found some good deals on remnants at Douglas Fabrics.

I shrugged, a little embarrassed. "It's been a while since I set up housekeeping in a house. I just thought I'd kind of enjoy it while I could."

"Hey, I think it's great." He looked at me intently. "So you're not afraid to have an address again?"

I had never told anyone about Tony's return, and I didn't plan to start now. "Time to stop running." I spoke firmly, and Drake dropped the subject.

"There's a bunch of mystery writers having a panel at Kepler's tonight," he said instead, not really looking at me. "Marilyn Wallace, Carolyn Hart, Linda Grant. Thought you might like to go."

It took me a couple of moments to realize that this was an invitation. From a man. They used to call it a date, I believe.

I had spent several years suppressing my womanhood, trying to be a faceless, formless neuter creature. I didn't know if I was ready to be female again. I still didn't have a hairdo, although I had moved up from Goodwill to the Junior League Thrift Shop. I was wearing decent jeans and a heavy cotton sweater, neither of them immediately identifiable as someone else's castoffs.

Drake was looking at me, a hint of anxiety in his eyes. He'd seen nothing amiss in my appearance. I could go out with him to Kepler's, maybe even buy a book new instead of secondhand. Or I could crawl back in my cozy new cocoon for a while longer—like maybe my whole life. Even if I couldn't take the stress of being a woman, surely I could be a friend.

"Sure," I said. "Let me comb my hair."